BACKLASH

PREQUEL TO THE WILDBLOOD

S. A. HOAG

Backlash
Prequel to The Wildblood

S. A. Hoag

Backlash: Prequel to The Wildblood

Copyright © 2015, 2025 by S. A. Hoag
Wildblood Ventures Books

This is revised from the original edition.

AI free zone. This book is 100% written by a human – me.

Cover designed by GetCovers.com

Formatting by Bob Houston

ISBN: 978-1-966538-00-4
CreateSpace ISBN 9781536968071
ASIN: B0104VMFI4

Reader Reviews of 'Backlash'

"Wow. What a prequel. Can't wait to get my teeth into the series proper."

"This was definitely worth the read. I would recommend this book to all who love this genre as I do."

"I like dystopian fiction, and this delivers in spades. A romp-through-the-wasteland read, with great characters woven in to make things interesting."

"Kept me reading to the end. Was a good introduction to the start of an interesting series. The development of characters was creative and drew you into their lives."

"I didn't find a dull moment in the novella. The story was full of action and suspense. More back story with the characters"

"This draws you right in from the first page."

DEDICATION

This one's for me.

CHAPTER 1

Sep 06   mid-afternoon   Montana

"What's out there?" Shannon asked her partner, looking east towards the derelict city. Miles from any place resembling civilization, they weren't there by accident. They chose the duty of guarding their home, a secluded valley tucked away high in the mountains. The snow-covered landscape and treacherous roads were the only things she'd ever known. Empty cities were ghosts of the past, and far more dangerous than they appeared from the distant highway overpass.

"To be honest," Ballentyne told her, leaning on the car, finishing a thermos of day-old tea. "I'm here to teach you to drive. That's all, that's what I agreed to. Then there's the fact you have a better idea about the outside world than the rest of us."

Shan snorted a rude word under her breath. "That's not likely. My team wants me to learn everything on my own. Security things, Scout things, and otherwise." The 'otherwise' being the catch.

She shared a mild psychic connection with her Guardian Team, Wade and MacKenzie. They privately referred to it as Gen En, genetically enhanced, a term they'd found in pre-war media. If it was true or not, they could only guess. The valley, The Vista, was closed off from the outside and had been since the winter after the war.

Their abilities weren't common knowledge. Those included in the close-knit inner circle had been made aware of the not-so-subtle differences at work in the trio. Wade had formed his own security corps outside the reach of Vista Security, to keep their secrets.

Ballentyne was one of the trusted few. He wouldn't get caught out overnight with a rookie, either, and especially not Vista Security's first female rookie. Not because of her sex, but because of who, of what, she was. All three of them had experienced unexpected side-effects to their abilities, a scenario he wasn't willing to deal with.

"What do you think?" he asked.

"I think there's more to the world than just us. Our parents have forgotten that." At seventeen, she had many opinions. Quite intelligent as well, Shannon understood not all of those opinions would pan out to be correct. "Someday," she said, throwing her pack in the back seat of the car and stretching. "Some of us should go find out. Off the record, if we need to." Tall, and more than pretty, she had a Mediterranean complexion, with green eyes and dark hair.

"Are you going to bring that up to Command?" Ballentyne wondered, amused. He towered better than a half foot taller than her. Mahogany skin, black hair and dark eyes, he'd been a Scout four years. Over the last winter, he moved to a Guardian Team, internal Security for The Vista, rather than driving circles in the mountains. At thirty something, he decided he was too old to be doing the hard footwork of a Scout. Half the people in Security were younger and better suited. This duty was temporary, a favor.

"I said off the record. I'm not in Command," she pointed out. As the ruling body of Security, they were officers and former officers, self-governing, and separate from Vista Council for many reasons.

"Wade is, and since you're their Scout, you will be soon enough. Mac too."

"You mean because I'm Gen En."

"That's why you're their Scout, Shan. If Command knows or not, you'll have to ask them." They had their own ways, their own secrets.

She had to agree.

"I'd guess Wade has ideas for something unauthorized like that," Ballentyne added, knowing his penchant for detailed planning. Wade was moving up fast in Security. Hell, rumor had it he'd been offered a future Council position.

"That's one thing I'm certain of."

"You're driving through Butte," he told her, back to the business at hand. Scout duty kept teams on the road for two or three days at a time, depending on the weather. The first line of defense, they were the eyes that watched for potential trouble from the outside world. In the autumn, cities became tenuous. Nomads started moving in for the season, while Scavengers never quit traveling. Both groups caused issues for Vista Security.

Shan groaned. "Is that an order?"

"Let's say it is. Concentrate on your surroundings. There are plenty of places to gather and this time of year, they're all migrating. That's why we have precise routes for the cities. Stay sharp and we'll be fine. The only movement we've seen in the past month is south. In a couple of weeks, we'll be set in for the winter, and it'll be months before you have to go back."

She'd driven the city with him over the summer and figured if she went there a thousand times, it would be the same. Cities were dead, abandoned places and had been since before she was born. The war, dubbed World War Last by children of the survivors, had emptied planet Earth of human inhabitants almost to the point of extinction. Few of those that remained could be called civilized. The Vista was isolated, for that reason.

"We'll be home by dinner," she recited what he said every morning he picked her up from Dispatch.

"I-90 in to Butte, I-90 out of Butte and we'll stop at Station One tonight unless plans change in the next hour."

"You're a brave man," she said, resigning herself to the trek.

"That's what I keep hearing since I volunteered to teach you to drive." She knew how to drive. He was testing her commitment to Security. They were both aware.

* * * * *

"I hope it's cold enough for everyone," Mac announced, stomping his feet like he'd been walking in snow. None was on the ground yet, but soon. The Guardian pair of Team Three came in from the underground garage, making their way to the main floor. The lodge had been part of a ski resort before the war, rebuilt and reinforced after. Now it was Station One, Vista Security's home away from home, and a favorite escape for younger officers seeking independence and a bit of privacy.

"If you ordered this weather, I'm kicking your ass," Denny Lambert yelled from the radio room. The temperature was below freezing, wind gusting in hard from the north, typical of any given autumn.

Everybody in earshot had a good chuckle. Unless they went three or four-on-one, there would be no kicking of Capt. MacKenzie's ass. Despite the laid-back cowboy look he dressed for, Mac could be deadly. With four years of Security experience, he was quick on his feet and quick into a fight. He'd be twenty-one at the end of the year, a couple months older than Capt. Wade.

Wade was the quiet one of the team. He grinned at their exchange, not getting involved, but still glad to be in for the night.

"Not me," Mac said, shedding his gear. "What's the plan?" Ten to twenty personnel occupied the station around the clock, plus up to a dozen civilians in support positions. No alert would mean they had time to relax for a few hours. Sex, drugs, and rock 'n' roll. Or at least dinner, beer and loud music per choice of whoever was in the comm center. Meaning the radio room.

"You can finish my shift," Lambert offered.

"Wishful thinking," Mac made an obscene gesture at the Scout stuck in Dispatch.

"Shan logged in a couple hours ago," Wade told him. The two men had the opposite relationship with their Scout. Wade was like an older brother to her. Mac was not.

"Outstanding," Mac answered.

"You got second shift tomorrow," Lambert reminded them. "Dispatch has us on Alert Six." All clear, no call-outs.

"Outstanding," Wade repeated. "Which commander is in tonight?"

"Niles. He traded off so Duncan can do some attitude adjustments at Station Two this week." Lambert shrugged, glad he was away from that drama. Council tried to nose in on Security matters from time to time. Station Two, in The Vista itself, had a couple of ringers.

"That's what I figured." Wade shook his head. He couldn't get away from this mess. His step-father was a founding member of The Vista and was on the Council. Council and Security were the core governing bodies of The Vista, separate but equal. There were occasional conflicts, and this was one of them.

"Not your concern. Forget about it," Mac told him.

"Until there's a foot of snow sitting on the ground, everything is my concern." Wade was in line for a promotion. The next step up would skip a rank to commander, likely by the end of next spring. He wanted to create a balance between Security and Council but was usually left wondering if it was even possible.

"So, are you taking your Scout out tomorrow?" Ballentyne, Mick in his off-duty time, peered down from the second floor loft, in civilian clothes, jeans and a tee-shirt.

"Is she ready to drive around by herself?" Wade asked.

"She's been ready all summer."

"We haven't been ready," Mac said, not joking.

"I'd rather sit in Dispatch with her than let her go out there, unprepared. I needed to be sure."

"Agreed."

"Let's not pretend both of us haven't shadowed her a few times when she was on her own."

Mac had nothing to disagree about.

"Give her the keys, tell her she's on regular rotation with us," Wade told Ballentyne.

"Are you sure?" Mac asked in low tones, keeping the conversation private.

"I should've put her on the road the week she turned sixteen, but I'd have had her parents and you to deal with. How she didn't make Ballentyne crazy over the summer is beyond me," Wade said, unwilling to just say he worried as much as any of them. "You want to keep her at rookie status another season? She drives you around in the mountains next, starting tomorrow."

"It's been more than a year," Mac said.

"We were both discharged from training status by the time we were her age. She knows she's getting stuck in Dispatch because she's a girl, and because it's what we wanted. Pretty soon, it's going to piss her off, and then we'll all pay for that indiscretion."

"Will Command release her once the season is over?"

"Because we did, they'll drag their feet and call Cmdr. Duncan in for his point of view, and anyone else that's worked with her. Us, too. We remind them we need a Scout before spring. She's got the routine down. The problem is, things have happened that aren't routine. That's why Security exists, but rookies are still rookies."

"Don't tell her I'd prefer her bored to tears in Dispatch," Mac said.

"In a perfect world, we should all be so bored. In this world, you and her and I have an advantage," Wade said. "We use that advantage every chance we get. She's smart, and careful. Let her do her job." Despite their abilities being unstable, they were still useful.

Mac nodded, agreeing. "If she knew, do you think she'd be angry?"

Wade stopped, furrowing his eyebrows. "Shannon, angry that you worry about her? We're talking about the same person, aren't we?"

"We are."

"I have to go sit at Station Two for Command and see if I can figure out who needs to be dismissed. Go tell her about her pseudo-promotion. Don't keep her out late. You're riding with her tomorrow. She's aware it's the end of the season, and we always travel in pairs when the weather changes."

Mac could think of worse duties.

* * * * *

"How long has the power been down?" Shan asked, awake enough to notice the safety light in the hallway blinked off.

"Twenty-five minutes, right after you came upstairs," Mac told her, shuffling around in the dark as quietly as he could. "It'll be daylight soon, anyway. When they get the system rewired, we'll be all good."

"Next summer," she murmured. The solar panels would keep the heat on but she curled up up next to him as he slipped in to bed with her. He felt warm, skin damp, like he'd just showered. "I thought we had a date."

"Until Dispatch sent me out towards Divide." He brushed her hair back from her face.

"I figured they found you a job. What happened?"

"Someone at the depot said they heard cars and since no one in Security was anywhere near there, they sent a couple of us out to have a look around."

"They sent cars out to see if there were cars out," she said. "And?"

"Nothing we could find."

"I'm not surprised." She'd learned over the summer that most calls led to nothing. It didn't matter how minor, someone always checked.

"We're not fooling around, are we?" he whispered. Even with thermals on, she was soft in all the right places.

"You have such bad timing," she told him. "There's a

rumor that I'm driving today."

"True thing."

Shan kissed him anyway, moving enough to make him groan.

"I'm pretty sure you just turned me down," he said, voice rough.

"Sorry," she offered, untangling herself from him.

"Don't be." They both settled in, getting cozy.

He hesitated again, and his uneasiness puzzled her. She was pretty damned sure he wasn't afraid of her parents, despite the jokes. It was something else. Team Three had a few secrets when it concerned private matters. Shan wouldn't ask, knowing she might not like the answer. It wasn't 'if', but 'when', and they both agreed on that.

"Are you worried about driving?"

"Not as much as you'd think." Drifting towards sleep, moving close again, she added, "Not as much as you are."

He stroked her hair for a while, trying not to imagine worst-case scenarios. Wade and Shannon were far more adept at the glimpses of emotion and insight the Gen En gave them. Mac struggled with the abilities they found easy. He kept certain aspects from them as well. It felt safer knowing they didn't tell him everything. Trust wasn't the issue.

"Shannon," he whispered to see if she was still awake.

"Alex."

Hearing her say his given name rather than his nickname gave him an adrenaline rush. "I'm glad you're here. I mean, not only here at the station, I mean in Security. All rookie harassment aside." He felt her lips curl into a grin against his neck. "Just don't forget I'm your senior officer."

CHAPTER 2

Sep 21   The Vista morning shift

"Well, that can't be good any way you look at it," Lambert observed as they parked across the street from Station Two. Shannon was driving. She needed some overnight hours, and now she had them. The sun was up and felt like it was going to be warmer than the past week.

Wade and Mac were waiting outside the station, standing on the walkway, looking bored.

"They haven't gone off duty yet," Shan said.

"Let's go find out why."

"Callout?" Mac guessed why they were wandering the streets so early.

"Yeah, Dispatch had a report of intruders out on the west loop," Lambert related the tale. "Turns out to be the Carter brothers."

"On the loop? On foot?" Mac laughed. It was almost four miles from town.

"They went on a binge and had been fighting, loud and in public, for about twelve hours. Normal for them, but you know how it is. People let us know about these little things."

"Were they as belligerent as usual?" Wade asked.

Lambert nodded. "The younger one? Clive? He pointed a gun at Officer Allen."

"Did you shoot him?" Mac asked her, a bit more serious. He'd dealt with them. They were harmless, even armed.

She just smiled.

"As soon as he saw she was a girl, he was all sober apologies and cooperation," Lambert finished. "We loaded them in the car and dropped them off at the hospital because if we took them home, they'd be drunk on the streets again by noon."

"So now they'll sleep it off, give the hospital staff a ration of shit, and be back on the streets in no time," Mac surmised the likely chain of events. "Same thing every other day until they get back to work." Their distribution center was closed because of a fire, and boredom was a real thing.

"That sounds about right," Lambert agreed.

"Let them walk home next time."

"Good idea," Shan said. "I run that far and it wakes you up, especially this time of year."

"You run? Miles? On purpose?" Lambert asked.

"A little over two miles, three times a week. In the snow, I ski instead, five miles whenever I can."

Lambert shook his head. He lifted weights now and then and counted cleaning his duplex as exercise.

"How long would it take you to pack?" Wade asked them, changing the subject, subtle as usual. Anyone that had known him more than a week understood how methodical he was. The question came with real consequences.

"Ten minutes," Lambert said without hesitation.

"For how long?" Shan countered, not as eager to commit.

"A week to ten days, on rotation with other teams."

"And what sort of facilities will we be staying at?"

"The depot in Dillon," Wade told her.

"An hour," Shan answered after considering it.

"We're going to Dillon?" Lambert wanted to confirm.

"We are," Wade said. "Command told me to get out there and start running shifts. First round of us goes out tomorrow after shift change."

"Who's going?" Shan asked.

"The usual, Taylor, Green and Ballentyne, Noel and Saenz, Ferretti, Jasso, Lambert," he said. "Team One and Five, at least temporarily. Keep in mind, not all of them are part of my security group. Mac and Lambert are going to round up the supplies we need. I'm taking you home to tell your parents the best reason I can come up with why you're going to Dillon."

"Michael won't have an issue. Deirdre, well, you understand my mother," Shan shrugged.

"I do, and that's why I'm going with you."

"Why are we moving out to Dillon?"

"Training. It's the end of the season and Command wants the rookies ready for next spring. Last chance to get some time on the road."

"So tell them that. It's no big secret," she said.

"Someone named 'Wade' is going to be pulling a shift in the comm room right off," Mac grinned, eager to get going.

"What bet?" she asked, raising an eyebrow. "If you owe Mac a shift, you had a bet."

"I said you'd jump at the chance to go. Mac said you'd play 'Twenty Questions' first."

Lambert laughed, seeing great humor in it.

"There weren't twenty questions, there were four."

"I said you'd go with no question."

"I wasn't questioning you, but the conditions. If I'm going to be out there, I want to be aware of what to expect."

"Expect to be doing a lot of driving." Wade already had a plan. It's what he did. "You'll have your own room, like most of us. You've been to the depot, you understand it's going to be crowded. Expect quick, plain meals, a warm place to sleep and more hours than you're used to. Expect to learn more in the next week than you have all summer. If I catch you slacking off or not doing your job, expect that I'll stick you back in dispatch for another year."

"You know me better than that."

"Why do you think a rookie gets to go?"

* * * * *

"Shannon," her radio crackled with static, snapping her out of a restless sleep. It was Wade; they had a private channel. Most teams did.

"Go ahead," she answered, groggy. Her watch read 9:30 pm, and she was supposed to go on duty at 2am. An hour— she'd been asleep an hour.

"Gear up. I'll be there in five minutes to get you."

"What's going on?" she wondered, rubbing her eyes.

"Don't ask, just do."

He didn't sound like they were playing war games. It didn't feel that way, either. Shan moved.

Her mother was in the kitchen. Deirdre Allen was five foot three, with pale blond hair, hazel eyes, and was one of The Vista's actual doctors. She'd been twenty-nine when civilization ended. "The hospital just called me in," she announced. "Are you on-duty?"

"I am now. Wade didn't say why."

"Training practice?"

"No," Shan said. "Not this time. I know you don't like carrying weapons, but I think this is serious. Take a sidearm, Mom, please."

Deirdre nodded. "For your peace of mind, I will." She

could use it; she'd had to in the past and hoped to never again. "Whatever it is, be careful."

"I am, and my partners wouldn't let me get away with anything else."

She hugged her. "I mean it." Most emergencies she attended to were Security officers.

"I'll see you when I can," Shan said, hearing a car. "That's Wade. If he tells me it's practice, I'll call you." She didn't think it was likely, but he'd fooled her before.

The moment she dropped into the passenger seat, she knew it was real. "Can you tell me now?" She'd dressed in winter camos with body armor, both Sigs and a boot gun, magazines in all her pockets, plus an array of knives. Her pack held spare ammo, helmet, face mask, food rations, fire starter, water bladder, and various other bits of survival equipment. The usual for team members on the move.

He glanced sideways at her, heading towards Station Two with a purpose. "We lost a Scout at Wisdom about an hour ago."

"Lost?" she repeated, not expecting it.

"DOA. They've called your mother in, too. This is a Security matter. Don't be exchanging information with her Shannon, not on this, not now. We can't tell what's happening out there yet. I'm going to concur on a Code Nineteen as soon as we get someone else from Command at the Station." They required three for such a drastic action.

Code Nineteen was a Blackout. It had been almost six years since the last one. "Where's Mac?" she wanted to know before anything else.

"He should be at the station by the time we get there. He wasn't out, relax." Wade could feel her tension with no effort.

"Which Scout?"

"I can't say," he told her, blunt as usual. "How many more questions are you going to ask me today? We're getting close to twenty."

She nodded, aware he wasn't angry at her. A Blackout was one step away from evacuating people. It put him on edge; it put all of Security on edge. Shan understood why. As a child, she'd seen the detonation on the Missouri Breaks. That Blackout lasted eight days. Luckily, The Vista was on the western side of the Continental Divide. Radiation drifted east in weather patterns.

Station Two had no place left to park. Downtown was the only area with wide, maintained lanes, and he abandoned the car in the middle of the street. "Keep quiet, follow my lead, don't do anything rash," he instructed.

"Got it."

They made their way to the comm room, already teeming with officers. She stayed close.

"Capt. Wade is here," Cmdr. Duncan spoke to someone on the radio as the rest of the officers fell silent. It was the first Blackout for most of them, and despite all their training, a layer of fear had settled in. "Go ahead."

"This is Cmdr. Perro, retired," he introduced himself. "Security Command."

"You're aware of the circumstances of the Code Thirteen less than an hour ago," Wade said. He never wavered, he never blinked. "Because we don't know what direction the intruders have gone, and the fact it's seventy miles from The Vista, I'm moving to issuing a Code Nineteen."

There was a moment of silence. "I agree," Duncan said.

"Agreed. Go to Blackout conditions. I'll inform the other members of Command," Perro made it official.

"Officer Allen," Duncan said. "I'll need a hand with dispatch. Someone that's qualified. Take a seat." He went on the air. "All stations, all teams, Central Dispatch, Cmdr. Duncan. Code Nineteen, repeat Code Nineteen. Stations and depots go to Blackout conditions, Alert Two. Secondary teams, return to your stations." To Wade he directed, "Get your partner and get to Dillon. We need someone watching the southern corridor."

Shan spotted Mac in the main room; he saw that look and nodded at her. They wouldn't get a chance at private words, not with a Blackout going in to effect. He'd call in their status later and she'd hear him on the air at least.

"Both of you," she told Wade. "Watch your backs." It was Security's way of saying be careful.

"We're going to play hide and seek in the dark," Duncan

explained to the rest of them. "Lead them away from here, away from Station One." Station Three was remote enough, it wasn't a worry. "You have your assignments. If you don't, step up and I'll give you one." The floor cleared as Security moved in to high gear.

Aware of protocol and having practiced over the summer, Shan got on the radio. If Duncan didn't approve, he'd tell her. "Central Dispatch, Station One, primary Team to the I-15, I-90 interchange." She paused for a moment. "Central Dispatch, Station Two, primary Team to the I-90 and Highway 12 interchange. Central Dispatch, Station Three, you are out of the target zone, Alert One."

Duncan stepped out to direct officers looking for something to do. "Car Eighty-Eight responding from here," he called to her after a few moments. Their high-tech office equipment included clipboards to keep track of who was where.

She didn't look to see which Scout had been south earlier, figuring she'd hear soon enough.

An hour later, after the first pass of Teams running routes, Duncan had everyone positioned where they needed to be. He took a seat. "You aren't on the schedule until third shift."

"No, sir," Shan agreed. "When I get a call to be ready, which shift I'm working isn't my first concern. Scout runs are three days long, not a few hours."

He nodded. "You're going to fit in with Team Three just

fine. I'll see how things have settled down at 2am. There are a couple people in the building that can work Dispatch. If you get too tired, and I mean too tired to be answering calls during a Blackout, say so."

"I will."

"Can I talk to you straight forward, Officer Allen?"

"Yes," she nodded, well aware Duncan wouldn't sugar-coat things for her. "Please."

"There were women in Vista Security before you, back in the beginning when we didn't have planned training or a defense for ourselves. You're the first woman in Security since we've developed those. It's been ten years."

"I understand not everyone is comfortable with me being in Security, and that my position as a Scout makes it more controversial. Some people would say it isn't safe." Shan thought of the many lectures her mother had given her. "Other won't believe I'm qualified and I'm sure there are those that think even less of how I got to be in Security. I don't care what people think. I've gone through the training, the same training as my male counterparts."

"You have and we wouldn't be sitting here talking now if you weren't qualified as a Dispatcher, and as a Scout. I've interviewed the officers you work with. Those are the opinions that count."

"Is this my training exit consult?"

"Part of it," he confessed, surprised she'd picked that up.

"I'm supposed to observe you while you work, during a code call if possible. Seeing that this is a Blackout, it's a little unusual. No, it's a lot unusual, but that's acceptable. Command has high expectations for you."

"I won't disappoint," she said, certain she could hold up to their scrutiny. An incoming call cut the rest of their conversation short.

"Code Eight, Team Twelve," a Guardian came on the air, hurried. "We're under fire, two miles south of Divide on the access road." They both stood to go to work.

"I've got this," Duncan said, calm. "You handle the Stations."

Shan nodded.

"Central Dispatch, Team Twelve. Team Three is south of you. Try to regroup with them," Duncan told them. "You got that, Team Three?"

"Team Three, Central Dispatch. We're five miles south, en route." It was Mac; it didn't reassure her.

"This is Central Dispatch, to Station One, Station Two. All teams standby, reserves standby," Shan announced. Her mother would hear her on the air and not have that worry, at least. The hospital had an officer on duty, and monitored calls. It was routine. Tonight wasn't.

"I know you want to be out there," Duncan told her. "Take a breath and do your job here. Soon enough, Officer Allen, soon enough."

"Blackouts don't happen every month, or every year," she said. "I'm damned glad for that, but yes, I want to be out there right now."

"This Blackout won't be over soon, not from the way things have gone before. Stay sharp."

The mood of the room changed a few moments later. "Code Thirteen," the call came in from Team Twelve. "We're under fire. There are at least six intruders. They appear to have ATVs."

"Get the secondary teams out," Duncan told her, going back on the air. "Central Dispatch, all primary teams respond to Divide."

"This is Central Dispatch. All secondary teams move to cover primary targets. Repeat, secondary teams go to primary. We are in Blackout protocol." She struggled to not fidget. "Reservists get orders from your Stations."

He switched over to the station's com system. "This is Duncan. I need qualified Dispatch officers on the floor now."

"Sir, I'm fine..." Shannon began.

"You're not being relieved; you're considered a secondary team. I want you patrolling the boundary of The Vista a minute after your replacement is here. You're not cleared to leave the city, Officer Allen. Tonight, an entire class of rookies is going to make sure no one sneaks into The Vista. In this case, it is absolutely not better to beg for forgiveness than to ask for permission – do you understand me?"

"Yes, sir." She was aware of the dire consequences for screwing up during a Blackout.

"Be very fucking careful out there."

* * * * *

At dawn, she crossed paths with her team again, as they were taking a break in the kitchen of Station Two. No one else was there. She wouldn't have cared anyway. Shan threw her arms around Mac's neck, holding on.

"I'm fine," he reassured her.

Wade let them be. The moments of comfort and peace were rare.

Pretty much everyone in Security was aware who they'd lost. The officer in Dispatch told Shan when she clocked out. Capt. Terry, to those that worked with him. A self-defense trainer for the teams, he got along well with nearly everyone. Two of his four kids were adopted and none were in their teens yet.

Team Twelve had minor injuries, considering all, but they'd be out-of-commission for a couple of weeks.

When she disengaged from Mac, Wade got the same treatment. "I was worried about both of you. Radio silence is bullshit."

"But necessary," Wade said.

She nodded.

"Tonight," Wade went right to the duty roster. "We're going to drive in shifts, around The Vista, like we do when there's too much snow. No one will be out on the roads. The last thing we want is to draw attention here. The other stations are locked down."

"Wait-and-see," Mac said.

"It might be an isolated incident. This time of year, so many groups in the outlands are moving. Nomads and Scavengers, and those that aren't either. It's not unprecedented for them to wander close. The attacks, those haven't been common for a few years, but it's only a few years. We take precautions, and, like Mac said, wait."

"What about now?" Shan asked.

"Home, and I mean our parents' places. Get some sleep, have a decent meal and a shower. None of us are at liberty to discuss any aspect of what's going on. I have a meeting with Command and Council. Unless something happens on the inner perimeter, we're shut down until Command says otherwise."

"What's the catch?" Mac asked. There was always a catch.

"In twenty-four hours, a group of us are going to head south, go to Divide and have a look around. A very specific group of us."

They understood.

"Do you think that will help?" Mac asked, knowing he'd

not be as aware, at least for the Gen En things they planned on attempting. They'd wander around the site of the code calls and see if they could sense any residuals–'ghosts', they called it, glimpses of events that had happened. It wasn't one ability he took to. He'd learned how to suppress ghosts, to ignore and push them aside. What he experienced wasn't the same.

"Can't hurt," Shan reasoned, not liking that he felt disconnected.

"When you two finish, go home," Wade said, making his way out. "Check in with Dispatch."

"Were you bored out there last night?" Mac asked.

"Not even a little, but we're not finished talking about what's going on tomorrow. Even if you contributed nothing that goes on between Wade and I," Shan tapped her temple, "Here, I'd want you for the support, because we never know what could happen." She was on the verge of anger. "That's not the case. When you're close, it's easier for me to sense things. Maybe you're a catalyst, or maybe it's because I trust you and Wade without question." Taking a breath, she added, "If you think you're not critical to the team, you're wrong. Deal with it."

He wrapped an arm around her shoulders. It wasn't easy to cuddle in tactical gear, but Mac made the effort. "Not what I meant. I didn't mean to piss you off."

"Just because you react differently to the Gen En doesn't

mean it's a bad thing. Someday we might figure it all out." She couldn't stay mad at him for long. "That's a lie I tell. It would be nice to understand what we are, but I don't expect it. Like all those dates we've missed."

"We'll have time alone soon."

"The time we've been trying to find for over a year now?" she asked. "It's damned frustrating."

"I know," he said, amused. "Believe me, I get it. Maybe we should run away and live in the Outlands for a year."

"I don't..." Shan turned enough to get closer. She scowled, considering it.

"What?" he asked. "You won't offend me."

"Let's not pretend you don't go out and get laid. I don't care about that. I'm aware of how you feel about us." She kissed him, slow, memorizing every detail of the few moments. "Sometimes, you need to say it anyway," she told him.

He did.

CHAPTER 3

Sep 22   Divide   noon

Wade paced the cold asphalt, trying to sense what happened a day earlier. He'd read the reports, but they were words on paper. This was different. Being on the scene might help him visualize the events so he could analyze them for himself. Even with the entire team present, he was drawing a blank. Ghosts most often happened at random, and only on rare occasions they'd been able to sense things on purpose. At best, their abilities were erratic, and this attempt wasn't moving.

Taylor shadowed him. It was his job–not regular Security, but the one he'd taken with agreeing to be Wade's right-hand man. He provided back up and an alibi to cover things that others might stumble upon. From what little they could find in pre-war media, Gen En things and civilians didn't mix.

"Anything?" Wade directed towards Shan.

"Nada," she offered, Green and Jasso sticking close, she

suspected, on Wade's orders. In theory, all three of them should be able to see ghosts. After that, they didn't know what to expect. From previous experiences, it was possible to lose track of what was happening in real time. They could ignore the sensation when it began, which came in pretty damned handy if they were in questionable company or driving.

"This might drag on for a while," Taylor said.

"Only an hour," Mac reminded them.

Taylor shrugged, "Sure."

"We're fifty miles from The Vista," Wade talked to himself. "And forty miles to Sheridan, but only twenty miles from Butte. Twenty miles from Butte."

"Station Three is a hundred and thirty miles out in the sticks," Taylor said.

Shannon crossed her arms and frowned at Taylor. He walked away, knowing better than to pick a fight with her. They were both still rookies, both in training to be Scouts, and their rivalry was amiable. The Taylor, Wade/Cameron, MacKenzie and Allen families had shared a house back in the beginning and their children had grown up together. Mac and Taylor had an occasional clash of attitudes, sometimes they all did. Out in the cold and the wind, not knowing where the enemy was and not understanding what to do next, tempers were short. Team Three—all of them—were in charge out here, beyond the boundaries of The Vista and the eyes of the Council.

"It helps his concentration to talk to him, direct his line of thought," she offered. "Don't annoy him." They were three of the five people that had seen the team work as Gen En rather than Security. Or they would be, if anything happened.

"What about you?" Green questioned.

She shrugged. "I've never found a pattern, or a trigger to what I see."

"Neither have I," Wade pointed out. "Mac is lucky enough to not experience the condition, not yet. We think it'll happen."

"Do you feel lucky?" Jasso asked him.

"On this, yeah, I do. A nightmare when you're asleep is bad enough. One when you're walking around, minding your own business..." Mac would pass on that ability at every opportunity, except today.

"That's not what it's like, not once you realize what's happening," Shan said.

"I've seen those few seconds before you realize what it is," Mac reminded her.

"I find it pretty fascinating," she insisted. "Seeing a piece of the past like you were there.

"Unless it's an ICBM," Green nodded towards the north, the Missouri Breaks.

"That was real, right in our backyard. I knew what it was, and I thought we were all going to die. When it's something terrifying, you can… push it away. Or at least Wade and I can. I don't speak for others."

"There are others like you, then." Green had always suspected as much.

"I meant Mac," she said, evading. The decision to take up that conversation wasn't hers alone.

"Are there more Gen Ens in The Vista?" Green asked, pursuing the idea. "Why would they hide from us when it's our job to keep them out of sight?"

"How would they know what we do?" Taylor asked.

They all looked at Wade. He considered the implications and where the conversation was about to go. "Since you're sworn to silence on all things Gen En, I guess knowing isn't any more of a burden than other things we've shown you."

"That doesn't sound good," Jasso said.

"I want in," Green said. "Taylor knows. He'd be jumping in the conversation if he didn't."

"There are others, other Gen Ens," Wade said. "I won't tell you how many or who. What I can say is that they're inactive."

"Meaning what?" Jasso asked.

"They're unaware of their genetic differences, and seem to have no particular abilities," Wade told them. "They're going on about their lives, as normal as we've had since the war."

"How did you find out about them?" Green asked.

"Officer Allen can sense other Gen Ens."

They all looked at her. "When I meet someone, the difference is as obvious to me as the color of their hair or the tone of their voice. We've watched several, and they exhibit no sign of the abilities Team Three has, or anything else out-of-the-ordinary." Shan made a quick story. "That's all I'm going to tell you."

"Are any of us?" It dawned on Jasso there might be a reason they hadn't mentioned it.

"No," Wade stepped in, knowing Shan wasn't kidding when she said she wouldn't disclose anything further. "We're not unique, but we are alone."

"That's not why we're out here," Taylor spoke up. "You can take it up again when we're back at the Station."

"If they're going to see ghosts out here," Mac said. "It should have happened. Now we're here to find out how serious you are. First, you get to hear how serious we are."

They all shut up to listen. Wade was notorious for planning out his moves. This was one of those things. They'd been expecting it for months, since Shan had gone on the road and Mac made his transfer to Station Two permanent.

"The 'Conda, the Anaconda Security Corp, has been an official entity in The Vista for a couple years now. Council doesn't like it, but Command has recognized us. With this attack, they have given us full access to Station Two," Wade told them.

"There's a good reason Security and Council matters are separate," Taylor said. "Council has gotten soft. They don't think the threat of intruders is as severe as in the beginning, or even a few years ago. It may not be, but easing up on patrols is a bad idea any way you look at it. The 'what if' factor is never mentioned when they start in on how Security is too big."

"We don't publicize everything that happens. What would the point be, when it would only split the public on believing us or them?" Mac knew there were things the two entities didn't share. He wasn't one of the chosen few in Command; Wade was, and Wade confided.

"My point," Wade told them. "I have been given authority to use the 'Conda in a Security capacity. We've taken over the search for these Nomads as of yesterday. I'm the liaison with Command. I'm in charge of this. Lambert and Ballentyne have already been debriefed."

"Damn," Green said.

"Ditto," Mac agreed. "This will plaster targets on us and Council will look to shoot us down. If you aren't interested in that sort of attention, now is the time to step away."

"But Command is covering our backs?" Jasso asked.

"Yes," Wade said.

"Council can make us miserable by calling us in front of them at every opportunity," Green said, knowing from experience. "They can't make me do anything, but unless you're willing to move up to the Siksika Ranchlands, you're out of luck." The Blackfoot Nation had existed four hundred years before The Vista, and continued to govern themselves much the same as they always had.

"It's an idea," Shan laughed. She'd worked in their communications center for training, a few times over the summer.

"Council is the reason Green is going to follow you around like a shadow until we get clear of this situation," Wade informed her.

"Do I have another option?"

"No."

"Fine." It wasn't so funny now, she decided.

Wade knew her well enough to understand 'fine,' meant things could be the opposite. She wouldn't take it up with him in front of the other officers. "If you want reassigned, talk to anyone in Team Three later. Right now, we're going in and deciding what's next. Get your schedules, watch your backs. This is more serious than wandering Nomads. We need to find out before this gets closer to The Vista."

overnight   Sep 24

"Want to drive?" Taylor asked.

"Where are we?" Shannon sat up, peering out into the dark.

"We'll be turning around at the Dillon exit in about five minutes. Fuel it, switch, and I'll get a nap."

"I wasn't asleep." Dressed in winter camos over body armor, they could have been twins. At any distance, she became indiscernible from her male counterparts, as long as she kept her face mask on and her opinions to herself.

"Looked that way to me," he said, smug about it.

"I was talking to Wade."

That made him think twice, raising an eyebrow. "All right, you win that one, Shan. What's going on?"

"Nothing in particular. Security is meeting on the other side of Glen at daybreak, so they can tell us what we're doing later today. They think a Commander will be in to see how things are progressing."

"Meaning we're being checked up on."

"Do you blame them?"

"Yeah, you can drive to Glen."

She fell quiet again, head against the seat, a faint static buzz in the back of her mind. Neither of her partners were attempting contact, but the communication was there. It often lingered; sometimes it was a whisper they couldn't quite hear. All three of them felt it at different times. Mac hadn't figured out how to respond yet. And sometimes, however insignificant it seemed, Shan and Wade both thought someone else was attempting to listen in, maybe even watching them.

Then she was wide awake, with the sensation like she'd had cold water thrown on her. Taylor was in the depot and she was sitting in the car, alone, in the dark. Pushing her door open, she moved to the driver's side, using the loudspeaker because his headset was on the dashboard. "Kyle, move!"

He did, sprinting out and throwing himself into the seat as she gunned the engine, sending gravel flying across the empty lot. Taylor snapped on his safety belt, cursing under his breath. "Code call?" he asked, not hearing any radio traffic.

"Not yet," she said. "Give it a few seconds."

A chill ran up his spine. "Should you be driving?"

"Yes, I should. Knowing what's happening a few miles away doesn't affect my driving, it's not like seeing ghosts."

"What's happening?"

"Code Eight, Glen cutoff," someone called, out-of-breath, answering Taylor's question.

"Code Eight, we're under fire at Glen," another officer

radioed in, shouting. "There's at least a dozen intruders, north and south of my position."

"Shit," Taylor exhaled.

"No response. We're in blackout conditions, no matter what we hear," she said, all the training they'd memorized seeming to mock them.

"Drive faster," he urged. Four more code calls happened in rapid succession, all of them Code Thirteen, officer down. Under normal conditions, there would be responding calls on the air. The silence was eerie. "What in the hell is going on out here?"

"I don't know. I felt it because Wade did."

"What?"

"Intruders. I'm not aware if he's on the scene or not. What ever happened, it was fast." Shan concentrated on driving. In an hour, they'd have daylight. For now, the dark was both their enemy and their ally, and her team was out there somewhere. She drove faster.

Within minutes, they could see the carnage. A security vehicle, abandoned and burning, sat halfway off the pavement, blocking one lane. For a moment, the blank readout screen on her dashboard lit up, then went to black.

"Did you get that?" Taylor asked.

"Yes. Get the Uzis, get ready. There are eight or nine cars over this next hill, and some of them aren't ours."

"Fucking wonderful. They have cars."

"Motorized vehicles of some sort," she said, turning the screen on. "Security shows up blue. Other colors mean not us. This isn't the first time Security has run across cars, just the first time for us."

He retrieved sub-machine guns from behind their seats. "There," he said, seeing cars ahead, and more fires. Being Wade's right hand, he also recognized that look, the determination, on her face. It was tunnel vision with all three of them, narrowing their concentration to the task at hand, and nothing else mattered.

"That's Wade," she said, not indicating which. "Car Four is Jasso, I think. Noel and Saenz are supposed to be out here somewhere. Mac and Lambert, too. I don't know the Station Two shift."

Muzzle flash erupted across the highway. "ATVs," Taylor said as a warning. "Maybe motorcycles or four-wheel drives. They're all over the place."

"They're scattering. That's not what we want."

"Pick a target, take it down," Taylor recited a mantra from training.

"I remember," Shan agreed with a slight nod, falling in behind several cars. North wasn't the direction they wanted any intruders to run. Security's job was to make sure they didn't get far. Their vehicles were reinforced with steel grills, side panels, and roll bars for a reason.

Gunfire peppered the Security vehicles, sparks flying.

One car spun out, leaving the pavement, and plowing up an enormous amount of dirt as it missed a stand of trees. For a moment, Shan thought it was going to roll on the steep slope. Then it did, going over once and a half before it came to rest on its roof, obscured by the billowing cloud of dust.

"Allen, get Green," Wade barked on the air.

"Hang on," she warned, braking hard and taking it off the road, the dirt shoulder slowing them down fast. Taylor didn't even have time to swear. She had her safety harness off before the car came to a stop. "Cover us."

He did, swinging his door open, using it to brace against, and wishing he had something bigger than an Uzi. There wasn't time to be digging around in the trunk for weaponry. Shan was out looking for survivors. Or one in particular, who kicked out his driver's side window to escape.

"Come on, Lt.," she urged.

He coughed and coughed, scrambling to get clear of the wreckage. "Fuck!" Green blurted out. The windshield had shattered, leaving him covered in glass shards.

"Are you hit?"

"No."

"Methane or refined?" she asked, worried about his fuel tanks leaking.

"Methane," he said as she got an arm around him, grabbing a handful of parka and pulling him away from the wreckage.

As they staggered towards her car, a third vehicle caught them in the headlights and Taylor was ready. "It's Mac," Shan shouted even before he jumped out.

"Get in my car, Taylor," he said, sounding like it was an order. He helped drag Green the last few yards and dumped him in the seat Taylor relinquished. "Harness," he directed.

"Got it," Green managed, in pain.

"Do not engage them unless you have to," Mac told her.

Shan caught his gaze, knowing him well enough to understand what he didn't say.

"Fatalities?" Green asked.

"Yes." Mac was honest with them. "At least three. Do not engage. Don't follow them into the city, either."

"She won't," Green assured him.

"You're a medic," Mac said to Green. "How bad?"

"Ribs maybe broke, concussion, I might need some stitches. Nothing that's going to kill me tonight."

"There are a couple of half-tracks and some artillery waiting on the interstate about halfway to Anaconda, if they go that way," he told Shan. "They won't leave the cover of the city, not during the day." Mac wanted to fight, but it was over. "We didn't let them go without their own casualties. Dispatch will issue orders as soon as they can. There's another incident site six or seven miles north. See if they need anyone transported and get him to the hospital. I'll be in after we clear this mess."

* * * * *

An hour later, the mist had turned to ice and left a sheet across most of western Montana. It wasn't uncommon, not even before the war, when the weather was less severe.

The car fishtailed as Shan pulled around the west side of the hospital, going faster than she should. A Station Two Scout was coming in behind her, transporting more injured officers. When Green quit complaining about her driving, she'd kicked it up a notch or two, not a damned bit worried about the other Scout's opinion of her driving.

Jumping a curb and missing the concrete barrier separating the lot from the river, she put the car in reverse and parked it as well as was going to happen. She honked and waved for an attendant. The emergency entrance was crowded with people, several rushing out in the rain to help.

"We've got him," a man she recognized as Dr. Roberts told her. "Are you injured?"

"Not me, Lt. Green."

"What happened?"

"He rolled his car." Shan couldn't think of a descriptive way of putting it. They were civilians. "He said he has a concussion and broken ribs."

Roberts nodded. Shan hadn't realized how bad it was until she saw the corridor lined with injured officers. "How long has he been unconscious?"

"Fifteen minutes," she said, stopping outside the double doors that led to the interior of the hospital. There was no reason for her to go in, not with so many in need of attention. It was a fear from her childhood. She'd been there so often with her mother and most times, all Deirdre could do was make her patients comfortable and wait for the end.

After a few more questions about Green, he said, "I'll let you know his condition when I can." Roberts disappeared behind those doors.

She stood there, wondering what was next, wondering where an uninjured senior officer was so she could get new orders and get back out there.

"Are you hurt?" Deirdre asked, emerging from one of the curtained-off overflow rooms. Beyond exhausted, it took a genuine effort not to grab her daughter and send her home. She wasn't a child anymore.

"No," Shan answered, going defensive when she knew she was going to lie. "I brought Lt. Green in."

"The officer from the Ranchlands?"

Shan nodded, seeing bloodstains all over the front of her parka. "It's not mine."

"Was he shot?"

"No, no, a car wreck."

Deirdre didn't seem convinced. "We've had a dozen gunshot wounds in the past hour. Dispatch told us to expect that many more before the night is over. Are we under attack?"

"No," Shan repeated. "I can't go in to details, I'm here, not out there. Just don't worry."

Waving her arm around at all the bloody and wounded, Deirdre said, "Don't worry, Shannon? You're aware we have deceased officers back there?"

"I am." Her voice sounded hollow, stifling any emotion that might burst out. "I have to go. It's not in The Vista, mom, we wouldn't let it get here."

Feedback from multiple radios stopped further discussions in the ER. "This is Central Dispatch, to all Stations, all Security Teams. Alert Four conditions are still in effect. Teams are to remain in assigned safety areas. Teams en route are to return to safety areas."

"Well hell," Shan said. They were all stuck at the hospital until further notice. She'd get new orders soon, she hoped, later if another incident happened.

"Go to the lab. We need blood donors and you're O-positive." Deirdre had to get back to work as the Scout following Shan arrived with two more injured. The Vista had a handful of genuine pre-war doctors and a growing number of those trained by them. Deirdre was the Chief of Staff. She might get a break before midday. It wasn't a bet she'd make.

A little later, Shan sat in the hallway near the nursery, out of the way, relieved of a pint of blood, when Mac found her.

"Interested in a closed meeting with Command?" he asked.

"No," she said. The one time she accompanied Wade, it left her with the distinct impression that Command had many things they didn't tell civilians, or rookies.

"I don't think it's an actual question. It's a request."

"Wade?"

"No. Not a thing to discuss here," he pointed out.

"City Hall, then?" Shan asked, always more curious than afraid.

Mac nodded. "I'll drive."

She snorted, "You bet you will. I saw the storm blowing in when I got here."

"You just gave blood."

"And?"

"It can make you light-headed. You crash into a tree, your mom kills me for letting you drive and, therefore, crash."

"It's never bothered me before." She stood, shrugging, picking up her gear. "See?" They headed out, taking a side door to avoid a myriad of questions.

"Sign a release form stating that," Mac challenged. He smiled and she let go of some of the tension that had been building for hours.

"No. Get in the car."

* * * * *

"Security has permission to operate in any manner necessary to find where the Nomads are based, and clear them out," Duncan announced to the group of officers assembled at Station Two. "We got the order a couple days ago, but with the events of last night, we're moving the timetable forward. Waiting for better conditions is no longer an option."

"Capt. Wade has chosen teams from Station One to accompany him to Depot South. He'll assign runs, the purpose to determine the number of intruders we're up against. Station Two is covering the inner perimeter; Station Three is running backup for anyone that needs it."

"How is this different from what we do every day?" Ballentyne asked what they all wanted to know.

"We aren't considering taking prisoners from this event, with the obvious exception of children and captives. It's organized, aggressive, and aimed at The Vista. By 'we', I mean Command. Team Three is leaving now, followed up by officers as assigned."

"Why Team Three?" Lambert whispered to Taylor.

"Shannon thinks it's a secret, Mac, too. Wade won't talk about it, but it doesn't take something extraordinary to figure out what he's not saying. Command knows." Taylor wouldn't say 'Gen En,' outside of a specific group, and Lambert didn't need a translator.

"We need to get this under control before we have civilian

casualties," Duncan continued. "None of you are being ordered to Dillon. It's a volunteer assignment. These are high priority targets now, not travelers, not outlanders, not Scavengers or Nomads."

"How long will Command keep these orders in effect?" Taylor asked.

"If we need to continue the search patterns on snowmobiles, we will. Until we find them, the Blackout is how we're living in The Vista."

Sep 25   Dillon

The wind started up from the south, and Wade paused, listening.

"What is it?" Force-of-habit, Shan waited beside him, her left hand dropping to her side and she unsnapped the leather safety strap from her Sig. She'd been his shadow, his bodyguard since before he enlisted Taylor, because of the idea someone outside The Vista was watching them. He was the most conspicuous in the team.

"If I knew for certain, it wouldn't bother me so much."

She rephrased the question. "Is it something I might have

to kill? Someone."

"Is that what you're worried about?" Wade shifted his attention to her, scrutinizing in a glance.

"No, not worried. I don't think… I won't flinch, I won't freeze, but afterward. What happens later?"

"You'll deal. You'll talk to someone about it like I have. What did Mac tell you?" They stood at the edge of the depot property, following a high stone wall that ran the length of a long driveway. It had been part of the resort, relics leftover from a time neither of them comprehended.

Shan frowned, wrinkling her nose and shrugging. "He said I'd deal with the issue."

"We will. If and when."

"We're all aware it will be 'when'."

"How long have you thought that?"

"Since the first time you had to."

Four years ago, at a place they called The Junction, twenty miles from The Vista. An active crossroads, Security still had issues there. Wade nodded. "Sometimes it's unavoidable. Civilization isn't what it used to be. We do uncivilized things, barbaric things, to keep everyone else safe."

"Isn't that how it's always been? With people, I mean. Our history is war."

"Probably, Shan. We chose the job. Sometimes, I wish you'd have followed one of your parents instead of me. I want you to be safe."

"I'm not afraid, but I want to know what's out there, in the rest of the world. So do you and Mac."

"It's part of the bigger plan, yes. We needed you trained in Security first."

"Count me in." She didn't have time to continue the thought, their radios beeping in tandem. "Oh, hell, here we go again," she said, glad for the few words.

"A code call," he figured. "Or they wouldn't put it on the air." They hurried back up the hillside, the urgency of the situation making their adrenaline run.

"Team Sixteen just got ambushed at Divide," Lambert caught them in the foyer before they could shed their parkas. "Mac's already en route with Jasso."

"Take a car, and go," Wade told Shan. "Lambert, you're with her. We're going to go see what we can." Then he was gone, heading for the front lot rather than the garage.

"By 'see', he means ghosts?" Lambert asked, hoping he had misinterpreted.

"That's what he meant," she nodded. "In the middle of a Code Call."

"Is that a good idea?"

"It's Wade's idea. Good or bad, we're doing this."

* * * * *

Resting her head on her hand, Shan leaned on the roof of the car and closed her eyes, enjoying the sun on her face for a few moments. The weather was cold, a perpetual condition, and warm days were rare. She wished they had a chance to enjoy it. They wouldn't, not today.

Wade was pacing the road, most of his gear discarded. Mac sat in the passenger seat of his car, having a breakfast ration. Lambert, Taylor, Green and Ballentyne were close, watching the perimeter, being the only other officers not sent back to the depot. They parked north of the scene, waiting. Team Sixteen had received minor injuries and would be home for a few days after the hospital released them.

Too quiet.

"Can I talk?" Taylor asked her.

She nodded. "Not to Wade. He's concentrating."

"Trying to find those ghosts again. What if Team Three didn't have the Gen En abilities, and we had to figure this out, anyway?"

"We'd wait at Dillon until it snowed and then track them." She'd had the discussion once already. Residual memories came in handy, if they happened. Otherwise, they were officers with a job to do. The weather forecast – calculated guessing – predicted snow in a handful of days.

"That might work," Taylor gave her. "But it also might take all winter and we can't sit in a blackout all winter. Four days is grating on nerves." His included.

And Mac's. "Aren't you supposed to be watching Wade?" He came around the car to stand with Shan, ushering Team Two over. Lambert and Ballentyne had taken a lookout.

Any inappropriate response, Taylor kept to himself. "Got it," he said, heading off to shadow Wade.

"Out of curiosity," Ballentyne spoke up. "What got Wade to have someone follow him around like this? It's not his style, not in his personality."

"Last year, Wade was in Council when a code call happened, and he knew before it came on the air," Mac told the story. "A public meeting with a hundred people. He faked being sick, but it made him evaluate the need for an easier way out of future potential problems. Now Taylor is his second, his right hand, to make sure little slip-ups like that don't become an issue."

"Does anyone follow you around? Or her?" Green asked out of curiosity.

"No reason to follow me. Shan, she doesn't like the idea, but Wade has been pushing it since she went on the road."

"That's why Wade wants us around," Green said.

Mac nodded. "He'll win that argument."

"In case of these little surprises," she agreed, wandering around the car, distracted, attempting to change her perception, to move sideways rather than forward. "Nightmares are just nightmares until the Missouri Breaks get nuked and we all watch the sky burn." It was a point, a sharp memory she used to focus on.

Mac let her, and they followed his lead. After a couple minutes, she stopped and stared north, shook her head, and started pacing. "Ask her what she sees," he whispered to Green.

"What's out there?" Green tried the casual approach, wondering why he got the task.

She wasn't ignoring them. A hundred yards down the interstate, Wade and Taylor were discussing what Command was telling Council. Shan heard them, she saw them talking like she was standing there with them.

"Shannon, can you see Team Sixteen?" Green asked, more direct this time.

"I can," she murmured. "But it's too loud." The men exchanged looks.

"The hell of it is," Wade was telling Taylor, "Council won't recognize this as a problem until The Vista is under fire. It's another Security 'incident', body count or not."

Shan felt time stuttered around her. She tried to move, to look up, the air itself pulsing as something massive blocked out the sun.

Ghosts, Wade realized, but too late to tell them. He was watching the road, before Team Sixteen left the depot. The roar of it was deafening; he could hear it because she could. He could see it on his own.

"Don't touch her," Mac warned, seeing her gaze go fixed

on things that weren't there now. Taylor was waving at them frantically. "They've never done this at the same time," he exhaled, alarmed, as the situation spiraled out of control in that moment.

"What do we do if Nomads show up?" Green asked.

"You're in charge of getting her away from here," Mac decided, pointing at Shannon, who was staring off towards the east, oblivious of them. "They can go defensive when they're like that and you interrupt. Be warned." He ran down the road to have words with Taylor, whistling for the others to join them.

"Have they done this before?" Taylor asked.

"No," Mac shook his head. "Not unless they decided not to tell us." It was possible. Part of their plans for Security included the idea that no one knew everything. That included all members of Team Three. "If we get company of any kind, you do whatever it is you do to snap him out of that."

"Clear." Taylor was aware when challenging Mac would cost him his career in Security. This was one of those times.

Shan struggled to direct her abilities, control them. The blackness overhead was disorienting, despite knowing it wasn't real. As it moved, it took form, passing overhead and heading south, changing, turning gray, becoming solid and real, an hour earlier. She sat down on the dirt shoulder, covering her ears until the noise faded away like distant thunder. When she looked around, Wade was crouched next to her.

"Did you see it?" he asked.

"Yeah, crystal clear" she frowned, too stunned to even swear. "What do we do?"

"We'd like to know, too," Taylor interrupted, impatient.

Wade stood up, still sorting it all out. He looked at Shan and she nodded in a silent agreement. "One, or was there two?"

Mac offered her a hand up and she took it, dusting her backside off while she thought. "Two," she answered. "There are two of them. We need to get to The Vista and get in the armory."

"For what?" Green asked.

"RPGs," Wade answered. "We need RPGs. They have helicopters. Two of them. The military sort, with big guns. The intruders on the ground are being directed towards us, by them."

No one had a smart-ass response.

"We need to get all qualified officers armed now," Ballentyne decided. "What do we say about the helicopters, about how we found them?"

"We say we spotted them heading south while we helped clear the area after the attack. Quick and simple." Wade didn't care what sort of discussions might happen later. Right now, he had bigger problems than rumors; two huge and armed problems. "Get on the video at the main library," he told Shannon. "I want an ID on what they are and what they're capable of."

"They were heading south," she confirmed for everyone's peace of mind. "They don't know where The Vista is."

"What makes you think that's true?" Taylor asked.

"They think we're somewhere east of Butte, maybe closer to Bozeman. They've been following the I-90 corridor looking in a search pattern. I know because I could sense it."

"I concur," Wade said. "And I-90 goes north, out of Butte." They all understood what that meant.

"Next stop, The Vista," Taylor said.

"Mac, go with Shan. It's late enough you'll be in town overnight. Stay at Station Two unless you hear otherwise. I'll let you know when to come out tomorrow," Wade said.

"Let us know?" Taylor asked.

"I'll use Dispatch so everyone can hear."

"You don't trust me now?" Shan asked, half serious.

"Don't pretend you can't make mistakes," Taylor said.

"It wouldn't be a mistake if I didn't notify other officers," Shan answered.

"Fucking helicopters?" Mac asked, voicing what they were all thinking, putting an end to a potential argument. "After all this time, there are helicopters? How in the hell did that happen?"

"Does it matter?" Ballentyne asked.

"Yes," Mac said. "It damned sure does." He was thinking

about the abandoned military bases dotted across the west.

"If they had The Vista on a map, if they knew where we were, they could be there, from here, in less than thirty minutes," Wade said, guessing. "We don't want northbound movement. A Blackout may not be enough this time."

CHAPTER 4

Sep 26   mid-morning   The Vista

"Hey," Mac put a hand on her shoulder, letting Shan know he made it back. He'd left her at the library long enough to change out of civilian clothes and get a fresh car. That was an hour ago. He'd been delayed at the station with a lot of questions he couldn't answer. They'd spent the night at their respective parents, having no other choice. Station Two, crammed with bivouacking personnel, was out of the question. He should have known better than to check in.

Shan, comfortable in the worn leather chair, trying to watch old DVD recordings of military maneuvers, looking for a match of what they'd seen, had the idea of falling asleep at the desk was a possibility. It hadn't taken much for her to lose concentration. Wade, doing no-telling-what down at Dillon, and they were stuck in The Vista again.

"What now?" she asked, rubbing her eyes. The library, with rows of rooms full of books, was one of her favorite places to spend a few spare hours. This was different.

"Did you find them?"

She ran the video back to a timestamp she'd marked. "There's this. Sikorsky UH-60 helicopters, called Black Hawks. They can carry up to fourteen people each. The armaments were anything from machine guns to missiles. A complicated piece of machinery. Some Nomad didn't jump in the thing and figure out how to fly it in a week."

Mac nodded, reading the same statistics she was. "A range of about 350 miles."

"They could be anywhere, out in the badlands, in The Park, anywhere. But where did they come from?"

"I wish I knew. We're running this information over to Cmdr. Perro, before we go to the station to get new orders. Be prepared to tell a lot of other officers you know as much as they do. We can stay with any parent willing to let us, until we hear the word to go."

"So we can sit on our... We're sitting on our asses," she complained, jumping up and swiveling her head to stretch the sore muscles she'd gained over the past few days. "All our training is for a reason, and it's not to be stuck in a library. If I have to stay here all day, again, I'll go crazy."

Mac grinned.

"Laugh now. I'm taking you with me."

"I'll save you the trip," Perro said, having come in through the side entrance and followed their voices. "Or at least, the one to see me. Crazy you have to deal with on your own."

Shan rubbed her eyes again, embarrassed. "Figure of speech, Commander."

"Ah, of course," he said. "I was your age once, Officer Allen. The world was different, but people haven't changed as much as you think. I understand your impatience. It's for the safety of everyone in The Vista. Including you."

They'd been lectured.

"Is this what you spotted?" Perro continued, meaning the picture froze on the monitor.

"It is," Shan confirmed, back to being serious. "Two of them."

He contemplated for a few moments, unclear on who had identified the intruders. Allen and Wade, certainly. When they were involved, so was MacKenzie. "I expect you to keep this information in Security. I mean the officers involved, and Command."

"Yes, sir," they answered.

"A panic is the last thing we need," he said. "You understand. Our people, the civilians we're sworn to protect, are here because they're survivors, fighters, strong and resourceful. And a few that are plain lucky. Unless it becomes an imminent threat, there's no reason to disrupt lives further. The Blackout has already gone a long way in doing that."

"We've been passing out RPGs this morning to qualified

officers," Mac said. About half of the officers were, and he didn't think it was enough.

"You're not qualified," Perro said to Shannon.

"No sir, I'm not even certain I've graduated from training."

"Cmdr. Duncan cleared you five days ago. Congratulations. Are you scheduled to go back to Depot South today? I'd like to pass on some information to Capt. Wade. The radio isn't as private as I'd prefer."

"If there's a code call, we're a secondary team today," Mac said.

"You can always order us to go," Shan offered.

"It's not urgent, Officer Allen, it can wait. Go about your usual business. Command plans to meet with all of Team Three when the opportunity arises. See what other information there is on these," Perro tapped the monitor, giving them a nod before he left the way he'd come in.

"I feel like they're checking up on us," Shan said, when they were alone again.

The code call went on the air before they could finish watching the video. "You've got to be fucking joking with me," Mac threw up his hands, exasperated. "We're going to be stuck in town again."

He wasn't wrong.

* * * * *

"Get that car into cover, Taylor," Wade warned on his handset. "We have company of the hostile kind, overhead and on the ground." There was nothing, no support, other than a handful of people, for miles and miles of cold, quiet mountains. Quiet, except for that helicopter.

Nothing was going through Dispatch. The moment Nomads moved, a Code Seven was announced and Security went stealth. It was standard procedure, even in the circumstances. Security had been making themselves visible and loud at Depot South, because it was south.

The helicopter circled wide, disappearing behind a stand of trees. They had four points east of the depot set up with officers and added firepower. The roads were rough, unmaintained in most areas, and the time it took to prepare was hours overnight. In a perfect world, they'd be able to draw it into the open and take it down. If the second one showed, and Wade hoped it did, they'd take them both and run the teams in a sweep to clear out any stragglers. The entire incident could be finished in two days. It was an optimistic outlook, and the one he was holding on to, however unrealistic it was.

"Coming back our way," Lambert warned, manning the southernmost point. Ballentyne was west, Saenz north and Wade east, with other officers hidden along the main road.

It had rained overnight, and a cold sheen stretched across the landscape; not quite ice or snow, but a slushy mix. Two cars had minor damage from collisions early in the day. The terrain allowed a certain amount of cover, despite treacherous roads and deteriorating conditions they were used to.

"Everyone get ready, stay sharp. We only get one chance at surprise," Wade told them. "If you're clear, aim steady and take the shot. We're going to show them we hit back."

"Overhead. Acquired," Lambert said, then silence.

Wade loaded a warhead into the tube, locking it in to place before stepping away from the SUV.

"Acquired," Ballentyne said, calm as usual.

"I can only hear it," Saenz chimed in.

"Shut up and aim," Wade said out loud to himself, concentrating on the sound. In moments, the helicopter emerged over the tree line, heading more northerly than west. Low, faster than he expected, and headed right for Ballentyne. "Mick, heads up," he warned.

The Black Hawk strafed Ballentyne's position, machine gun sputtering, and either jammed or ran out of ammo. Pulling up, the helicopter headed east again to make another run at him, gaining altitude.

"I'm clear, keeping in the tree line," Ballentyne announced after several long seconds. "They didn't spot me."

"When they come around, they'll drop to follow the highway again," Lambert said. "I've got the shot if they do."

The helicopter took its time to circle around. They all held their collective breath, thinking it might break off and continue east. Past their outer perimeter, out in to the badlands and no one in Security would follow them, not yet.

"Heading west, take the shot," Wade said, hoping to hear an RPG launch or Lambert announcing his intent to fire next. Blood pounded in his ears and a line of sweat traced across his forehead despite the cold. There was only so long he could hold the intense concentration it took to watch the target when it was out of his line-of-sight.

"Fire, fire, fire," Lambert called out, and a moment later, the RPG spiraled towards its target as the helicopter swung around ninety degrees to evade.

As it gained altitude, the missile hit. The explosion lit up the overcast sky, sending debris in all directions, some pieces large enough to be dangerous.

"Check in, Lambert," Wade called, worried. Almost overhead, from his perspective. "You still with us, Denny?"

"Hell yeah!" Lambert shouted. "Part of that shit landed on my car." He was panting like he'd been running, adrenaline getting the best of him.

"Stick with protocol until we can clear the incident scene and be certain the second helicopter isn't close," Wade went right back to being in charge. "Nomads are on the ground, too. Let's not forget that. Point officers meet at Lambert's position. The rest of you stay put. If you notice anything, anything unusual, shout it out."

"I need a ride," Ballentyne said.

"Saenz, get Mick and come on over."

"I can't even fucking brag to my girlfriend," Lambert grabbed Wade, slapping him on the back the moment he got out of his car.

"You're right," Wade said, breaking out of the stone face he'd been wearing for days. "Nice shot, by the way."

"Lucky shot," Lambert confessed. "When we practice, targets don't fly like that."

"We'll have to talk to Command," Wade said. "Later, when we're locked down for the winter. When we have the other helicopter on the ground."

"We should go find out if there are survivors."

"You just want to go get a closer look at what's left of the thing."

"Don't you?" Lambert asked.

"Yes," Wade responded, retrieving an Uzi from his trunk. "Let's go see."

"Hell yes."

* * * * *

Shan drank a shot of whiskey, stuff older than she was. Stifling a cough, eyes watering, she rasped, "That's smooth."

Mac preferred Scotch and matched her shot. He didn't cough. "One down, one left." He was excited, more than he should be, considering they missed the entire situation. "I'd like to go to the scene. Figure out the logistics of it for myself." Both had suspected what happened from the flurry of officers rotating in from Depot South. It wasn't a guess, and there wouldn't be confirmation yet.

"You've seen helicopters before," Shan pointed out, peering around to be sure no civilians were in earshot. The club had only a handful of people, being in a blackout. "There were a bunch over in Missoula, most of them military. Billings, too, and I know you've been to the airport in Butte."

"Yeah, with caravans picking up supplies. We knocked this one down, though." He wished he'd been there. That she'd have been there with him wasn't a pleasant idea, and he had second thoughts.

"Want to know who gets the prize for this?" she smiled, teasing.

He regarded her for a moment, trying to decide if she was joking or not. "Guessing, or something else?"

Shannon tapped her forehead, then waved at the bartender for another round.

"How?" he asked. "You haven't been asleep."

"I don't always have to be. I felt a massive rush of adrenaline and poof, I knew who launched." She didn't have to go into deep details.

"One shot?"

She nodded, still grinning. This chance was gone, but she

intended to be there for the next one.

"Not Wade."

"Nope, not Wade," she confirmed. "Denny."

"Huh, good for him," Mac said, meaning it. "My next guess would've been Mick." He also was their large arms expert.

The bartender brought their drinks, two of the same. "There are ten minutes before they call the curfew. I live upstairs, and unless you want to sleep in a booth, you need to get moving." He turned around to announce to the handful of people still milling around. "Curfew calls in ten minutes. Drink up now."

"Drink up now," Mac repeated, doing just that. "Noon shift tomorrow, primary team. We might get into some of the action. I have my doubts, but maybe."

She drank her whiskey, didn't cough and jumped up. "Oh, we're going. I'm out for now. I'll see you first thing." In the morning, she meant, knowing full-well he'd be in Dispatch the moment the curfew lifted. Sooner, if anything happened. "Unless you want to stay over. It's a closer walk." Her car was parked in the underground garage at Station One, along with the rest not in use.

"Are your parents at home?"

"They are."

He considered the invitation. It wouldn't be the first time. When he stayed, it was in her room. Wade had as well, but everybody understood they were platonic. Well, everyone except for her mother.

Shan found it ironic there was more concern about Wade's reputation than the conspicuous interest between her and Mac. She'd let it lie.

"I'll pass tonight. I've got a stack of books I want to go over."

"What sort of books?"

"The sort that might help us with that current security concern." He didn't memorize, he remembered.

"Ah," she understood. "Get some sleep, Alex. I won't listen to you growling at me all afternoon because you stayed up all night."

* * * * *

Sep 27   6pm   The Vista

"Central Dispatch, to all local teams. Will someone please go out to the barricade on Frontage Road and pick up Officer Juno? His wife is in labor and wants him there an hour ago."

"Dispatch," someone not identifying themselves responded. "Please keep the air clear in case of a real callout."

"You go to the hospital and tell her," the officer came back. Everyone was on-edge, waiting for something to happen.

"I suppose our little side trek could have been worse," Mac made small talk, ignoring the radio drama. Escorting a caravan out to the Ranchlands broke up the tedium of their afternoon, for most of an hour.

"Please, please, let us get rotated back to Depot South," Shan said. They'd already driven the route through town, around the city limits and along the access road three times. It was getting late, and they could take a break.

"They might send us after nightfall. Wade wants us out there. Command wants Wade happy. Therefore, we get rotated as soon as he gives the word. And after this..." he shrugged. "Back to the same old, same old."

"I get a lot of reading done in Dispatch during the winter," she said.

"Don't we all?" he asked, and they both laughed. Boredom was the in-joke of Security, and there were a lot more cold months than busy ones.

"Getting stuck at Station Three doesn't bother me. There's a pretty extensive library they salvaged."

"Maybe we'll get lucky and be out there together, now that you're officially our Scout."

"Promises, promises."

"Central to all teams, all Stations. Half an hour warning to curfew," Dispatch interrupted.

"My place or yours?" Mac asked.

Then the car died. They were clipping down the road

doing fifty, a nice easy pace on a road she knew well. The car slowed, not even sputtering. "Fantastic," Shan's voice ran the full spectrum of sarcasm with a single word. She pulled to the side and stopped. The car merely clicked when she put it in park and tried to start it.

"Pop the hood," Mac said, climbing out. She did, following him around to stare at all the parts, wondering which was broken. "I don't suppose you've taken any classes in mechanics."

"The same as you."

"One." The single class all Security officers received in the basics of car maintenance. He checked the battery cables first. "Try it now."

Sitting back down, she turned the key, and the car clicked again, almost mocking them. "It's not getting any power. The dashboard lights aren't even on."

"Alternator," he guessed. "Turn on your headlights and try to start the car." He paced a few feet out in front to watch. The lights dimmed as she tried it. "That's my best idea." He came back and sat in the passenger's seat. "And here we are."

"Call it in. We're ten miles out and have five minutes of daylight," she recited a saying from security circles. "Maybe we'll get lucky."

"No chance," he said. Then, "Car Eleven to Dispatch." During active incidents, they used car numbers rather than team designations, in case anyone of the unfriendly sort could hear them. The voice mods made everyone sound alike.

"Central Dispatch, Car Eleven, go ahead."

"Code Fifteen, six miles north," Mac answered.

"Negative on the Code Fifteen. No tow available."

"It's going to be damn dark by the time we walk in," Shan said. "Not to mention cold."

"There are some new houses about a mile over there," Mac told her. "We push this dead beast off the road in to cover, get our gear and camp there until they can send someone around in the morning."

"Good enough," she said, gathering her belongings. Between the Ranchlands and The Vista, they were safe, but stranded.

"Central, we're going to get in cover on Aspen Park Drive until daybreak. Put us in for a Code Fifteen again, if you would," Mac told Dispatch.

"First thing after curfew ends, Car Eleven," they replied.

"Have someone notify our families we're just stuck out here with a dead car, please."

"Will do."

It took them half an hour to get the car into the trees and hike over the hill to the line of houses being built. Most were unfinished, and they picked one in the middle of the block. All occupied homes and most other buildings in use in The

Vista were at least partially underground, with the exception of the downtown areas. New constructions were as concealed as possible because of all the things they feared. Those reasons didn't seem so trivial now.

After a quick perimeter check, they hauled their gear inside and began setting up for the night. "Find a cozy spot and get the windows covered," Mac directed, finding a corner to prop an AK in. He locked the outside door and started arranging their gear. It would get cold overnight, but not so cold they were in danger of frostbite. The solar disc heater would stave off the chill.

"This one is as good as any," she said, dropping her pack. Setting her AK down, she tacked up the heavy curtains she found folded beneath the window, complete with hammer and nails. There was a loaded Colt 1911 and three spare clips on the pile of supplies as well. "Did you bring anything to read?"

"Always," he said. They never knew when they'd need temporary entertainment. Books were the preferred choice, portable, convenient, and didn't require a power source that might work. The heater would give off enough light to read by. With the blackout, their radio was pointless, but if a change in the alert happened, it would be broadcast. "Hungry?" he asked, unrolling his sleeping bag.

"I'm not." She wasn't and wouldn't be until they were in The Vista. Wound up and ready for days now, with no place to go.

"Don't pace, Shan. Sit down, relax, enjoy the few hours of free time you get."

"Okay, Mom. I don't like being stranded."

"No shit. I might never have realized that."

"Smart ass." She arranged her bedroll next to his, tucking a blanket in the bottom and fluffing the small, flat pillow by beating on it. Then she settled in, digging a book out of her pack.

"Herbert," Mac said, peering into his pack, revealing the author without telling her which book.

"King," she countered. "The one you think of first."

"I'll raise you a Bradbury."

"I've got…" she went through the various items packed for such an emergency. "A pack of dice, some sugar cubes." Shan pulled a stray book out. "Ah-ha, Zane Grey."

"Trade me."

She gave him the paperback. "I'm good for now. I think this is Wade's pack, because I know I didn't pack a western."

He smiled, getting comfortable. "Imagine how irked he'll be when he goes through your stuff. Romance novels and tea bags."

"Not my fault." She scooted down into the sleeping bag, taking off her handguns and setting them aside, within easy reach. Then her boots, followed by a lot of squirming around, then body armor. "I should've done this first."

"Good idea," Mac said, discarding his. "You can't sleep in body armor."

"Have you tried?"

"No, and I'm not tonight, either."

"Chicken," she said after a few moments.

"Tomorrow's going to be a damned long day."

"I hope it's not a boring day." She smiled at a stray thought, setting the book aside to close her eyes for a few minutes. Just a few minutes to rest.

When Mac woke, her sleeping bag was empty, sidearms still on the floor. No emergency, certainly. He made his way through the house to the porch. He knew she wouldn't sleep well, but her stealth surprised him. "Everything all right?"

"Sure. Insomnia," she answered, gazing out in to the night. The sky, clear, glittered with stars. Shan was leaning against the porch timber, keeping under the awning, in the shadows, wrapped in a quilt she found in storage.

"Nothing going on with Wade?" He joined her stargazing.

"Not that I'm aware of. Just awake. I'm usually driving around on my shift."

"You should try to get some rest."

"I sleep during the day, you know that," she said.

"What aren't you telling me?"

"We've had this conversation. Every time we do, you forget it three days later. Sleeping next to you when we're alone isn't easy." When he shook his head, she reached up to catch a handful of unruly hair and kissed him. Mac leaned in, hands on her hips, and drew her against him. The kiss lingered.

"Do you think now is a good time for this?" he asked.

"You said it. We have twelve hours of dark, twelve hours of curfew," she said, knowing they'd just passed the autumn equinox. "When are we ever going to have this much privacy again, Alex?" Not wanting to hear an answer and not waiting for one, she kissed him again, swaying her hips against his. "Don't say no. Say yes and mean it."

"This is crazy," Mac whispered.

"This is the only thing the past week that isn't crazy."

"Yes."

* * * * *

"You two get the second floor dayroom, for however long this break lasts," Cmdr. Niles said, tossing a skeleton key to Mac. High tech stuff in the station. "Get some sleep. You're on-call now and on-duty at 2pm. Capt. Wade wants you at Depot South by dark." He was gone before either could respond.

"It's about time. I feel like we're a well-traded commodity," Shan said.

"Right now, I think all Security Teams are. Don't let it go to your head." Mac told her, wondering if the kitchen had anything prepped.

"I meant it as a compliment, sort of."

"Don't let it go to your head," he repeated.

They dropped their gear in the dayroom. Half a dozen sofas lined the walls, as Station Two had been bivouacking officers for a week, scattered equipment about, from backpacks to sidearms to a fold-up tent. There was even a saddle in the corner, left by some unlucky rookie that got stuck on a mounted patrol in the city overnight.

"Set that beeping alarm-thing-from-hell that you wear for noon," Shan shook a blanket out. His watch had woke them an hour before daybreak. She found pine needles in her blanket and didn't know how they'd gotten there. "I want a shower. I want a decent meal. Depot South won't have either."

"They're getting supplies, but don't expect great accommodations." He set the alarm, crawling onto the nearest couch. "If it needs to be said..."

"Yes, Alex, I'd like that." She curled up in her blanket on the sofa next to him, smiling. They whispered for a while, until they both fell into an uneasy sleep.

* * * * *

"This looks like something dumped out the back of a semi," Shan said, surveying the lobby of the depot. Same problem as the dayroom at Station Two, multiplied.

"Worry about where we sleep later," Mac said, unconcerned. "We need to be here."

"I know, I know. Keep it simple. The maintenance crew is going to hate us after this."

"I'll tell whoever is manning the radio to let Wade know we're here." They'd grabbed rations and ate in the car on the way out. The support staff had been sent to the safety of The Vista a week ago.

Picking an uncluttered area near the side entryway, she arranged their equipment in a neat a circle, wondering where everyone was, and if they were having any luck hunting.

Mac popped back out of the radio room a few minutes later. "Come on."

"What's the plan?" Shan followed him out the main doors, feeling like they were chasing shadows.

"We're going to find out in a minute. From the looks of it," he said, meaning the number of cars in the lot, "We all get to drive tomorrow."

"Alone?" she asked. Out of protocol, but authorized. If she didn't get artillery, it wouldn't be a surprise.

"I'd give the order. More of us trying to draw their attention away from The Vista. Get them out in the open. Take care of the problem at the source."

"Do we want to challenge an attack helicopter in a car?"

Wade pulled into the drive before he could answer. "Let's

ask him," Mac suggested, wondering himself.

"Are we going to go play chicken with a helicopter tomorrow?" Shan asked, arms crossed over her chest, as he joined them.

Wade considered how to answer that before he did. A simple 'yes' would only elicit more questions. "We lure them out and get a clean shot. Same tactic we used on the other one."

"Lure them out," she repeated. "Mac said the same thing. Do you mean all of us?"

He nodded.

"Do I get an RPG?"

"Have you ever fired one?" He didn't need to ask if she was qualified. She wasn't. Neither were a good half of the officers at the depot.

"Never."

"No, you don't get one. We can't afford a miss, or for you to blow yourself up trying to figure it out."

"So if it gets on our tail, we try to out-run, out-maneuver a helicopter? I read the specs on those things and that won't happen."

"I understand," Wade said. "The groups running together will include at least one qualified officer. All we need is a few seconds to get it in our sights, and it's over. Blinds are set up all over the perimeters. You know where they are. They're designed to keep us out of sight of travelers, and are perfect for hiding from a helicopter. We have the advantage of knowing the terrain."

She looked skeptical.

"Do you trust me?" Wade gave the standard response when she challenged him.

"Of course," she sighed. "You're the one that told me to question everything. Including you."

"Mac, are you going to go out towards Sheridan and help flush this thing out?"

"No doubt about it."

"Are you in, Officer Allen, or do I send you home in the morning?"

Uncrossing her arms, she put her hands on her hips. "I thought this was a volunteer operation."

"It is," Wade confirmed. "That's why I asked."

"If you didn't want me here, you'd have left me at Station Two. You know I'm in. Try to send me home." It wasn't so much of a challenge as a statement.

"Everyone is in debriefing as soon as curfew is called. Then we go to work."

"Against the curfew?" Mac asked. "Good idea, to get set up overnight and be ready for them at first light. Not as good a sneak attack as the first one, but it might work."

"Like we already did once this week. The bad news," Wade directed at her. "You're sitting in the radio room for the first few hours. Before daylight, we'll switch off and get Team

Three out prowling."

"I can do that."

"Good. If something happens overnight, in the dark, I want you on the radio."

"Let's do this," Mac said, tapping his ear bud. "Dispatch called curfew."

"First thing, and it's between us as friends," Wade said. "This is our chance to prove Command isn't just putting blind faith in us. We're out here to do a job, to face an enemy that no one expected. It means we take chances, we do things we wouldn't do in other circumstances. I'd rather chase them all winter than have either of you get injured. I guess I'm saying, be careful."

"This can't get to The Vista," Mac said. "We're done being targets, even if that's what we want them to think. Stick to our training, but use those abilities we have."

"Yes," Wade agreed. "It doesn't matter, out here, if someone notices. That brings up my second point," he said to Shannon. "Mac and I chose these teams after a long discussion. If you have a problem or a hesitation about anyone, we need to know now. Your instincts about people are as good as ours, maybe better."

She hadn't worked with all the officers at Depot South, but she knew each of them. "I have no issues."

"Last point. We trust each other." It was all he needed to say.

* * * * *

"Where did they go?" Lambert asked on the air. The highway was deserted. He could see miles down the mountain and it was void of human activity.

"Do you have any movement?" Wade asked, concerned about the erratic pattern they were traveling. The Nomads were going in circles, backtracking, cutting cross-country. At least eight, in reality, more. The thought he had, that they figured out Security was searching for them. After all, they'd lost an entire helicopter.

"Nothing here," Lambert said. "You?"

"No, and that's a problem. We had them minutes ago."

"Heading west because they can't go north."

West, Wade thought, trying to get a sense of things around him and for a moment, he had perfect control. He could see across the valley, hear sounds miles distant. With all the unmarked dirt roads and doubling back they'd done, he understood one thing for certain — the Nomads were heading towards Depot South. They were close, if they weren't there already.

"Allen and Green," he called on all channels they were supposed to be monitoring. "Respond." The static seemed to stretch on and on as he waited for an answer.

"Go ahead," Green answered after a few moments.

"You've got Nomads on your doorstep. Get out of the depot." Wade knew he'd understand the order. "Evac now, repeat, evac now. Do not engage." There would be no answer. "All teams return to Dillon, Code Seven." In half an hour, he'd find out if he realized what was happening soon enough.

"Shannon!" Green yelled down the hall. "We have company of the hostile kind. Evac orders."

She met him in the main lobby, already shrugging on her vest. "Evac?"

"Wade said 'Nomads on your doorstep'. You know how much he doesn't exaggerate."

"If we run and they just waltz in here, is there anything that can point them to The Vista?" she asked.

"Nothing," Green said, grabbing a pack. She had one, too. "Not in any of the depots. You know the protocol."

Glass shattered and there was a loud thump as something broke through the window opposite the fireplace and clattered to the floor, flames spewing out.

"Fire bomb. Basement," he spun her around and urged her towards the rear of the depot, realizing the other doors were likely covered by hostiles. The sub-level connected to another section of the old resort that was demolished years ago. It was a hidden exit now.

Shan eased the heavy door open, 9mm in hand, knowing he was still recovering from his rollover. Green stood to the side, weapon drawn. "Looks clear," she motioned. They both moved, low and silent, out into the dark, fifty yards from the depot.

It wasn't as clear as they thought. Riders on horseback were coming down the main driveway, too close for comfort. Green pointed to the tree line, across an open field. Cut back twice a year as a firebreak, there was no cover. "Do we go for it?" she whispered.

"They're going in the front of the depot," Green said, watching them. "As soon as they pass that curve in the driveway, we're out of their line-of-sight. Then we take the chance and run like hell."

They did, too, slipping away in the dark, following the treeline to get a better view. Shan stayed in the shadows, eyes on the intruders, Green right beside her. "There's more of them than I thought," she said, understanding why Wade had said to run. The Nomads continued to hurl fire bombs through windows on the main floor.

"Shit," Green spat. "We're going to lose the depot and there's not a damned thing we can do to stop them."

"What now?" Shan asked, ready to follow his lead.

"We wait for the teams to get here," he said, not about to go against unknown enemies in the dark, not if he could avoid it. "Never try to beat the odds when you have backup coming. There are a couple dozen of them and two of us."

"Hey," a rider coming from the opposite side of the depot

called out, spotting them.

Both drew weapons and Green directed, "Hold your fire," as he double-tapped the Nomad. "Go," he told her, heading into the pines. "If we get separated, keep moving. Head north and find the teams on the interstate."

"We won't get separated," she told him. "Not on accident."

Green acknowledged with a brief nod. "I forgot how well you do during night maneuvers."

"Nothing unusual," she said, keeping up with him. "I pay attention and practice." Discussing her abilities with someone not a teammate wasn't a thing she did.

"That's one point of view," Green said. "Not the consensus, but an opinion," he went on. "We can play hide-and-seek all night out here if we have to. Is Wade close?"

She could sense it in the air. "He is."

"They won't sit back and let Nomads burn us down without a fight."

"Good," Shan said. "We should take some of them alive and find out where the other helicopter is, find out how they learned to fly them."

"I'm sure that's the plan." Green looked back towards the depot. Flames were reaching through the windows, casting odd light in the trees. A few of the intruders were moving into the forest, looking for them.

"From the north, too," she whispered. "They've got us cut off from the road."

"As long as it's dark, they'll never find us in here," Green told her.

"They're going to open fire to flush us out," Shan warned, looking for an escape route, spotting a pair of Nomads with Uzis.

"Up," Green said. "Get up a sturdy tree, now. Quiet, quick, try not to break any branches."

Holstering her handgun, she looked around and grabbed a low branch, pulling herself up. Green followed. Ten feet off the ground, he got a hand on her butt and shoved, urging her higher.

"Watch it," she muttered.

"Unless you prefer to get shot tonight, stop worrying about me grabbing your ass and climb," he told her.

One Nomad fired a quick burst into the trees, encouraging their upward trek. She stopped when she had to, when the branches started getting too thin to hold them both. They were over twenty feet up. Green motioned for her to move down to a sturdier limb, placing himself right next to her. He was shielding her and hanging on to a thick branch, knowing he might catch hell for it later.

The trigger-happy Nomad wandered under their tree, oblivious. Neither of them dared to move or breathe. A falling pine cone might end it all. Shan stared straight ahead while Green watched the intruder. "Clear," he said after minutes passed. "Draw your sidearm. Get ready. There are more on horseback following the game trail." He armed himself as well. "Do what I say when I say it."

"Understood," she answered, still staring.

"Are you afraid of heights?" he asked, alarmed at the sudden idea.

"No," Shan said, looking at him. "I tracked that last one. He's back up on the access road."

"I believe you," he said, knowing the distinction between 'tracking' and 'watching' when it concerned Team Three. His voice dropped. "Riders. Where is Wade?"

"Closer than he was. Are you all right?"

He nodded.

"You just climbed a tree with broken ribs," she said.

"Bruised ribs," he corrected. "As soon as the teams get here, the Nomads will run and we'll get out of this fucking tree." The difference between Nomads and Scavengers was simple. Scavengers were uncoordinated, savage and unpredictable, while Nomads ran in groups. These were organized, the idea floating around in Security being that this group was military.

"They haven't been running."

"Point taken," he said. The fire from the depot was apparent from their vantage point; the building engulfed, sending a pillar of smoke a hundred feet into the night sky and lighting up the entire area. "They've set themselves up, parading around the depot like it's a bonfire party."

Shan saw what he meant. Easy pickings for a sniper. Or a group of officers sneaking up on them. As the wind shifted, they heard gunfire on the far side of the depot, the pop of small arms sounding like toy guns from a distance.

"Ammo in storage."

"The wind is coming up and blowing this way," Shan said. "We need to get out of the tree and back up to the road, if we have to engage or not."

"Wade said not to engage and I agree."

"Did he mention getting trapped in a forest fire?" she asked. Embers from the depot were falling around them. They'd both seen massive fires caused by simple lightning strikes and it had been a dry month.

"Not that I recall," he said. "Don't break cover. I mean it. We'll have a look around and decide what the best option is."

"It's dark," Shan said.

"Yeah, thanks for that. I wasn't sure." Green waited, watching and listening. The depot compound was big. It was going to burn for a while.

"I've been an officer for a week. I get it, that I don't know what I'm doing out here."

Green shook his head. "I've never been burned out of a depot before, either."

They moved down a branch at a time until they dropped to the ground, Shan first. Green followed, then heading north, knowing they'd be safer if they kept off the trail.

It only took a few minutes of fighting the uneven ground and thick growth to wear him out. "Slow down," he told her. "Don't get too far ahead." She'd been right. Climbing had taken a toll on him.

Loud music erupted from somewhere close for a few moments. "That's Vista Security," Shan was relieved and excited at the same time.

"We're not breaking cover," Green replied. "Not yet, not until I know we're clear."

Shannon didn't have the chance to tell him they weren't.

Nomads came out of the shadows. The one closest to Shan swung at her head with a length of PVC pipe and she had just enough time to throw her hands up in defense. The brunt of the blow hit her left arm, and she went down, trying to roll away from her assailant. She caught a glimpse of Green, putting up a fight against two more of them. The good news was that he was a hand-to-hand combat instructor; the bad news was that he had broken ribs to begin with.

"This one's a girl," the Nomad wielding the pipe at her announced.

"Then don't damage her, you idiot," one yelled back.

Shan drew. As the Nomad turned to her, she shot him, a double-tap to the center of the chest. The force flung him back, and she came up fast, aiming at the closest of the pair. Green was struggling with him and in her line-of-fire. She paused, waiting for a clear shot.

Wade stepped in before she had the chance and took out both Nomads in the space of two heartbeats; head shot, heart shot. "Clear," he called out.

She checked the closest Nomad, making certain he was dead. Without a doubt. "Clear," she said.

"Intruders due south," Green warned, catching his breath.

"My car is on the access road." Wade motioned back the way he'd come.

"I'm taking point," Shan said.

"We're not running from them," Wade said. "We're leading them right out where we can pick them off. Round up a couple and interrogate them." When Wade said 'interrogate', he meant it. Until now, he'd kept Shan away from some of the harsher aspects of life in Security. She wasn't stupid. She understood how they dealt with intruders. Tonight, she'd see some of those things first hand.

When they made it back to the blacktop, Wade pointed out where he wanted them to wait, out of sight, for a few minutes anyway.

Green stopped him. "You saw what happened?"

"We discussed this when she started out on the road and a few days ago when the Blackout was called. She's Team Three, she'll be fine."

Green was unconvinced. "What if she'd been alone when they caught up? What happens when she's alone, out here, and runs across more people, more men, like these?"

Wade took the time, a precious few moments, to consider what to say. "What I can tell you is that she's not in as much danger as you think from random Nomads."

"Convince me," Green persisted, angry and more afraid for her than himself for that moment before she opened fire.

Rubbing his eyes, it was obvious to Wade his Scout had picked up her second. He'd suspected it earlier, and this confirmed it. "You understand what happens when we see ghosts. It's not the same, but we have a defense response, and it creates a delay in their reaction. It's a reflex to a threat, not something we control."

"You know she can do this?"

"I do," Wade said. "Again, we can't do it at will. It wouldn't affect you. She could have taken out the three of them without that ability. She's Close Quarters trained, like you are, but we haven't gotten around to getting her certified."

"Because of the Blackout."

"It hasn't helped. This is one of those details we don't need to speak of. She became aware of them before either of you saw them. I felt her reaction, I saw where you were, I stepped in. Sometimes, that's how we work together, and tonight was good timing."

"Why are you telling me?" Green asked.

"You're going to be her second. When we don't have a firefight about to blow up all around us, we can get the details of that on the table. Right now, cover her, cover me, try to keep up. I'm tired of dealing with these Nomads. They're going to find out how big of a mistake it was to come at us."

"Hey," Shan popped up from looking in the trunk of Wade's car. "We got big guns." She helped herself to an AK-47 and a pocketful of mags, plus a heavy scarf to conceal her features a bit.

Wade shook his head. "We want at least one of them alive. Two or three would be better. Try to remember that when they come through the trees, Officer Allen. There are Vista Security officers out here, too. Use your sidearm first, please."

True to his prediction, a handful of men came down the same trail, noisy and hurried. They glanced around at their surroundings before rushing onto the blacktop, certain their prey had taken flight. The car sitting there startled them.

Team Three was no one's prey. Wade strode behind the front quarter panel of his car, barking orders. "Drop your weapons. We have you covered by snipers and close-quarters shooters." He held an Uzi, to make a point.

"Bullshit," one Nomad, an unshaven blond man of about forty carrying a myriad of facial scars, challenged him. "One car doesn't carry an army. There are two or three of you." He held a small caliber handgun. It was still a weapon.

"Go ahead," Wade told him. "Call me on this. You'll die surprised." Even as he spoke the words, he knew they were going to fire on his team. He swung the Uzi up.

The Nomads fired. Green returned fire in tandem with Wade. Three fell, including their apparent leader. One ran, and two others dropped to their knees, hands up in surrender.

"If there are more close by, that was a call for help," Green said.

"Agreed. Watch them," Wade directed, bolting after the fleeing Nomad.

"Shoot both if either even twitches," Green told Shan. "I'm going to search them." He checked the dead first. It took him a couple of minutes, tossing guns and various knives as he found them. As he finished, there was gunfire somewhere up the game trail.

Wade came back alone. "Let's make this easy for all of us," he told the remaining pair of Nomads. "Tell me what I want. We drive you out to the badlands, you go south and never come back this way."

"What if we got nothing to tell you?" one of them ventured.

"You've killed my people. I take it personal, like you were the one pulling the trigger. Lie to me, refuse to talk. I beat it out of you, because I can do that. Trust me, you wouldn't be the first or even the tenth. That's my job, that's why I'm out here." He paused for effect. "After you talk, I shoot you in the head and this is all over." Wade leaned close, intimidating. "I know all about the helicopters. Right now, I want to know where the other one is. I want you to tell me where you came from. If you have misplaced loyalty to people who've left you here to die…" he shrugged. "It's all the same to me. I'll be in a warm bed by morning and you'll be in a shallow grave."

Neither Shan nor Green had a thing to say. They kept watch. Wade stepped back for a few words with them.

"Captain," Green acknowledged, aware that Wade wasn't bluffing.

"Officer Allen, I'd prefer if you take my car and go watch the access road for our reinforcements," Wade told her. "I won't make it an order. You understood this before tonight."

She squinted at the fading fire beyond the trees. "No, Capt. Wade, I can't."

"Are you sure? One of them will talk. It will get bloody here, and I don't want you involved in this if you have any hesitation."

"It's your call, like it or not," she told him. "If I left and more of them showed, that would be my responsibility, leaving you without backup."

"Never a word, not even to Mac."

She tilted her head, signaling she understood. "What if he knows anyway?"

"It would be intangible," Wade reassured her. "If he questions you, send him to me. If what's about to happen is too much at any point, I want you to go. No judgment."

* * * * *

"I know you can sleep in a car," Wade said. It was the mainstay of Scout duty. "You've got a little over six hours before first light. Go to the campsite at Twin Bridges, get some rest."

"Who?" Green asked. Shannon was driving, Wade riding shotgun, while he occupied the backseat. None of them had much to say.

"Both of you. I'll be sending other officers up there as we clear the depot." What was left of Depot South, he meant. "We're taking that last helicopter tomorrow."

"Where's Mac?" Shan asked, exhausted.

Wade gestured to a row of vehicles that had converged on the area. "He's here. Say 'hello', say 'goodnight' and go," he told her. "You need to stay sharp. We all do. They did this to confuse us, and to scare us. They accomplished nothing but to piss me off. I'm not alone."

"Can I get an RPG?" she asked, figuring it was worth one last try.

"I want a helicopter intact, but that's not happening. Neither is the RPG for rookies only allowed out of the dayroom this week." An exaggeration, but not by much.

Shan nodded. "Fair enough. Shoot first this time."

CHAPTER 5

Sep 29   before 6am   near Sheridan

A tapping sound woke her, and Shan sat up, wondering where she was for a moment. Backseat of her car, covered in a blanket but not much in the way of comfortable. Mac stood outside, a cup of what she hoped was hot tea in each hand. Broth, soup, or even the chicory blend they called coffee would do. Something. It was cold, faint light beginning to show along the eastern horizon. It was always cold.

"Are those for me?" she asked, getting out of the car as gracefully as she could manage.

"One of them is," he offered her a cup. She took it. "Wade told me to wake you up and say we're on today."

"Good," she decided after a moment and a sip of lukewarm tea. "I'll be ready in ten minutes."

"You have thirty. Grab breakfast. Someone has a mess tent set up over by the creek. We'll find you soon."

"Do we have a plan?"

He raised his eyebrows. "You need more sleep. Get ready to go."

Shan nodded, heading off to wash up and then find a meal. It turned out to be dehydrated rations, maybe eggs and bacon and maybe not. At least it was a hot meal. She was aware it might not happen again soon.

Overnight, they had lined the cars up under the trees, hidden beneath camouflage netting, and stashed a batch of supplies in a cave on the west side of the camp. Fresh snow covered the neighboring peaks, not much higher in altitude. Winter was perpetual.

Soon, the rest of the officers gathered, Wade arriving with Ballentyne and Jasso. "Let's do this," he announced. "You've got your individual assignments. The basics. Drive around in the open. Kick up clouds of dust, be noisy, draw attention. The second you hear or see something out of place, any Nomad, any sign of that helicopter, you announce it to everyone. There's cover every few miles, you have them marked on your maps, and you should have them memorized if you've driven here more than once. Use them."

"Question," Lambert said. "They're on the ground, too. Is the helicopter our primary target?"

"That will depend on how this plays out," Wade said.

"They might have the idea to trap us on the road while their air support moves in. The order still stands, that you are under no obligation to take hostiles as prisoners. Defend yourself, however necessary. The helicopter is top priority, yes. If you have a shot, take it. If it swings around to start a run at you, hide. Get into the trees, away from your vehicle, and stay there. This isn't routine for any of us. Don't be shy. Call for help." Wade knew they trusted his judgment. He wasn't about to betray that confidence by missing this opportunity. The Nomads were nearby and bad weather was setting in. "We move in ten. Line them up," he gestured towards the cars.

Wade beckoned for his team to join him. "If we sense anything early, fantastic," he said. "If we don't, no big deal. Read nothing in to it because it's not a concern." They both nodded. He handed them maps with new checkpoints hand drawn in. "You know the routes, the side roads, the abandoned buildings along the way. Keep sharp, take nothing for granted. Let's go drive around and see what we can see. You understand what I mean. Shan, you're out first, Mac two minutes later, me five minutes after that."

Mac caught her hand. "Wait," he said, wrapping his arms around her. "I'm going to be close, damned close, all day long. If you think you need to call us, then call us. Even if you want to just say 'hi'."

"You don't want me to be out here," she said rather than asked.

"I wish you weren't. I wish none of us were. You're as qualified as any officer to deal with a helicopter."

"I suppose I am."

"Be careful. If you get that urge, if you need to run, go."

"I will," she said. "The same thing applies to you. It's appropriate for Team Three to bail the hell out if there's a helicopter involved."

* * * * *

"I'm fucking bored, I'm fucking bored," Shan recited over and over, drumming her fingers on the steering wheel as she headed south on Highway 287 again. Her fifth pass; a rough ten miles south, turn around, ten miles north, three miles west on a side road, turn around, three miles east. Do it all over again.

Deirdre had always told her profanity wasn't ladylike, so she tried to do less of it. Not that she cared if she was ladylike or not. Her mother could make her feel guilty over anything, and that was one of those things. Shan was relieved Deirdre didn't know what was going on and wouldn't have a reason to get into the classified reports later.

Shan glanced at the radio and announced, "I'm fucking

bored." She didn't have to put it on the air for Wade to know. So was he, so was Mac, and every other officer wandering up and down the roads around Sheridan. Nothing was out-of-the-ordinary this morning, not a trace of any activity that wasn't theirs. The sky was clear, with some high, wispy clouds to the north. She tried to imagine the Black Hawk circling around so someone could get a clear shot. It didn't help.

"What's the time?" Green asked anyone who wanted to respond. He seldom wore a watch and the one he'd packed for this trip to Dillon had burned in the depot, along with the rest of the gear stored there.

"Call it 9:30," Mac replied.

Shan smiled to herself. Both her partners were at ease for the moment, a good sign considering they were hunting a helicopter through the icy mountain roads.

"Jasso, take 41 north for about ten," Wade started switching them off. "Lambert, make a run around the old airfield." They didn't have to answer. "Officer Allen, stay on your regular route. You and I and Mac need to meet up. I'll tell you where in a few."

It was something different, anyway.

True to his word, Wade came back on the air with orders as she was turning around. "Allen and MacKenzie, rendezvous with me at the bottom of The Roost." A scenic overlook south of Sheridan, and Scouts used it for just that. "We may move the search area."

"Clear here," Ballentyne let them know.

An icy sensation crept up her spine minutes later, a physical sense, not some imagined, fear-induced paranoia. It made her ears ring and her adrenaline race. Shan realized where the helicopter was, and it was behind her. Moving in from the reservoir, maybe even Yellowstone. Wade hadn't said why they were changing their search pattern, but considering they didn't all head south at daybreak, she doubted he'd been aware. Not a guess, but one of those things they couldn't define, and he'd been right. Too late, but right.

"Imminent Code Seven," she announced on the air, dead calm. The others would understand. "Three miles south of Robber's Roost. It's the Black Hawk. I can sense it coming in from the lake, I think. It's going to intercept me before I get to the lookout."

"You've got a V8 in that car and you're a Scout," Mac was on the air and not so calm. "You floor it and find a place to fucking hide…"

"Officer Allen, we're minutes away. You can handle this," Wade cut in. "There's a subdivision of old houses ahead off to your east. Find cover until you have support. Green,

Ballentyne, Jasso, Taylor, get to the Roost. All other officers continue on your assigned routes." Wade considered the Nomads had people on the ground, close, looking for trouble. "Keep your eyes open, people. They're waiting for the helicopter to cripple us so they can move in."

Shan did what Mac had urged, pushing the car on the unmaintained road. Paved and level to a point, and a hell of a lot less dangerous than crossing paths with a military helicopter. "I see the houses," she told them. "They look like they're falling down." She got her helmet on, preparing to run.

"You need to shelter, not move in," Wade answered. "Can you see the helicopter yet?"

"I can hear it," she said, turning off the main road and heading for the houses. "Collar mic, I might lose signal," she warned, wanting to get as close in as possible. The subdivision had never been finished, and the road was an obstacle course of broken pavement. There was no good place for cover. "I'm out of the car and heading for the nearest house." She pulled into a row of pine trees that had long ago overgrown the sidewalk, throwing the car into park and bailing out. The Black Hawk buzzed overhead, low and fast, banking hard. "Shit," she said to herself, knowing they'd seen her. She snatched the AK from its rack and ran.

The uphill path and frigid temperatures slowed her down.

By the time Shan made it to the first construction site, she felt like someone had kicked her in the chest; no pain, but a deep ache from the icy air forced into her lungs. Swinging around, she stopped and planted her feet, firing at the chopper as it passed by again. A sniper fired back, their armaments not working. More likely, she speculated, they were playing with her, just to see her run.

"I said hide, not engage," Wade repeated. "That's an order."

"They started it," she answered to herself, looking for cover. The first house wasn't much more than a skeleton, the building showing years of rough weather. She made a dash for it anyway, dodging a pile of broken concrete. Pausing, she waited for the helicopter to swing out and turn. As it did, she sprinted to the next house. It was more completed, but still not much safety. She had no chance to move on to another. A landslide had taken out a section of the subdivision during the last monsoon season.

"I'm in sight of The Roost," Ballentyne announced. "Five minutes."

Shannon wondered if she had five minutes. Her side twinged from the exertion. As she tugged the body armor back in to place, she noticed a sticky patch along the edge. "Shit," she exhaled, examining the blood on her hand. It was hers and fresh. Their sniper wasn't as awful as she'd imagined.

"How bad?" Wade asked, knowing, a tingling itch beginning across his left side.

"It doesn't hurt yet. I don't know." Shan told him, a burning sensation starting. "I think it caught me under the edge of the flak jacket." When she stopped to shoot back, she figured.

"How bad what?" Mac asked, helpless, the emotion of stark fear catching him and not letting go.

"A scratch, a ricochet. I'm okay."

"No one panic," Wade said. "We have a medic en route."

"I'm close," Green said.

"Helicopter east of me," Taylor said. "I'm on the county road and Jasso's in my dust. His radio might be out again." They were closer, but on a dirt road.

"They're coming back," Shannon said, fleeing farther into the interior of the house. The mounted machine gun screamed to life, and she threw herself on the floor as parts of the house splintered and sent shards flying in all directions. She found only a framed out back half of the house as she scrambled away. She made it to the deck, losing her headset. As the Black Hawk passed overhead, she caught two or three rounds in the jacket, slamming her into the wall. When the helicopter circled around again, she'd have nowhere to hide. Throwing the AK over the side, Shan jumped off the deck, despite the ground sloping away. She hit the frozen ground hard and rolled up under the deck, seeing stars and trying to catch her breath.

Then the helicopter strafed the vehicle racing up the highway. Wade's car. He could see lead splattering into the pavement in front of him, almost as if it were taking place in slow-motion. It wasn't. He swerved as the car took multiple hits. Both left tires blew, and the car spun sideways into the gulch that followed the road.

"Shannon," Mac called. Then, "Wade."

"I've got Wade's position," Ballentyne said. "Someone get up on the switchbacks and take that damned thing down."

"I'm there," Green announced.

"Green, go to the second switchback. I'm right behind you," Mac told him, in charge, with Wade off-the-air. The switchbacks, the dirt road, was on the opposite side of the hill, higher ground. "Cover us."

"I've lost visual on the Black Hawk," Taylor told them. "Heading southeast."

"Stay at the bottom of the overlook, Taylor," Mac said. "Jasso too, just in case. All cars, hold your position until further notice. Keep in cover." He hit the first corner too fast, skidding in the dirt, the back quarter panel glancing off a tree. It didn't slow him down. Shannon's car, abandoned on the street, did.

"I'm out of the car. I may lose radio contact," Mac said. "Ballentyne, if they blow me to hell, you're in charge." With the radio turned to all frequencies, he started a dialogue with whoever was out there, listening. "If you can understand me, Black Hawk pilot, come on back here and shoot at someone that can defend themselves. Or are you just a chickenshit with a dangerous toy?" He had the trunk open and locked a warhead into place, hoisting the launcher and waiting. Listening, trying to use those Gen En abilities he knew he possessed. He'd qualified to use the RPG two days ago.

"It's coming back," Shan whispered, knowing Wade sensed it and hoping Mac did. It hurt to breathe; she wasn't certain if it was her or Wade.

"Helicopter south," Ballentyne warned.

"I see him," Mac said to no one in particular. "Let's dance."

"Keep it steady," Wade said, stuck in his car, with the doors jammed shut. He could smell gasoline and smoke.

For a few moments, it looked like the helicopter was going to turn back south. "Run away now, and we'll still find you later," Mac said on the air. "I promise."

"They can't hear you," Shan shouted across the road at him, making her way over.

"Stay put," he yelled back, seeing the helicopter bank

towards them. "Stay out of sight."

"Shoot it," she urged.

"Out of range," he replied, getting ready.

"What's the range?" Shan asked, needing to sit down from the exertion of walking up the hill.

"Two hundred yards max. The less the better."

"They jammed their machine gun. That's why they haven't run at you." She sat down, dizzy. "The sniper is pretty fucking sharp. Hit me at least once. Don't let them get overhead."

"Great," he said, keeping his attention focused even if he had confirmation she was injured. She was also mobile and talking. "Here they come." Mac watched it weaving back and forth, moving fast. Five hundred yards, then three hundred, then two hundred. "Heads up, live fire."

Shannon passed out a moment after she watched the warhead hit the Black Hawk, almost dead-center. As the missile detonated, she thought how it looked like the fireworks adults in The Vista sometimes set off for holidays that used to be.

* * * * *

"She's aspirating out into the mask," someone shouted. Shannon couldn't see anything and their voices sounded distant and hollow, as if they were yelling down a long corridor. "Roll her on to her side. Her lung is collapsing."

"Where's Green?" another voice called, one she recognized as Mac. He was holding her hand, and she squeezed it.

"Wade's hurt, he's trapped in his car and it's burning," Ballentyne came back.

"The helicopter is down," Mac yelled. "Call a Code Thirteen, damn it, before we lose the whole team."

* * * * *

Oct 05   Station Three   White Sulpher Springs   mid day

"There are a few points we should discuss. All of them concern you and the unique abilities of your team," Perro cut right to it. He'd driven himself to the Station as soon as the Alert Six, all-clear, went on the air. Command had been busy recruiting Mac after he led Security to rout Nomads at Dillon four days earlier. He was aware, even with Wade being the designated Team Leader, Mac was the first of them to join Security, and was directing them towards specific goals. It was subtle, and he wondered if the other two even realized.

Both Mac's partners were recovering in the infirmary, the

east wing of the Station, away from the prying eyes and endless questions they'd be subject to in The Vista. He'd spent three nights sitting next to Shannon while she slept, with the hourly trip across the hallway to look in on Wade. After another few days, they'd all be itching to go home.

Civilians wouldn't hear the word 'helicopter'.

"Is this the same debriefing Wade got a year ago?" Mac asked.

Perro regarded him for a moment. "Not quite. But then, you aren't Capt. Wade."

Mac shook his head. "I'm the odd man out concerning Team Three."

"No, but you are different."

"Different from you, or different from my team?"

"Both," Perro said.

"I'm Gen En," Mac felt defensive. "You might know more about us than we do."

"I wasn't aware of what you called it, or if you even acknowledged the abilities you've developed. You're not like your team, or any Gen En in The Vista. It's not as unusual as you imagine, because each of you are individuals. All of us are. It might tie you to one of the early corporations that experimented with human genetic manipulation. They were far ahead of the ones that came even decades later, but that information has been lost in time."

Mac was uncertain about what any of that meant. "Enlighten me, Commander."

"As best I can. The things we discuss will be private, and I mean between you and me, not you, Command, and your team."

Mac nodded. "I recognize there are things about us Command knows, because some members were involved."

Perro tipped his head, neither denying nor confirming.

"Are we human?"

"Yes, of course."

"Why am I so different?"

"Again, it goes back to who altered your genetics. Because they didn't understand the science of DNA as well as they believed, engineered traits reacted in ways no one expected. The fact is, I know little about you, other than your genetic markers are altered. Does that mean anything to you?"

"No, it doesn't," Mac told him. The fact was, now that he'd verified it, he had a starting point to learn more. "How did you become aware of these things about us?"

"I can't say where the information comes from. We want

all three of you in Command, and in time, that will happen."

"To what end?" Mac saw there had to be a point to it all.

"Being in Command and current Security Officers, you can carry out missions no one else is qualified for. Missions Council is uninvolved in. Our ambition, our plan for the next five to ten years, is to establish a community, one that will be outside the influence of the Council."

"Can we do that?" He asked, having the same idea from plans circulating in Security before he joined.

"Any village or outpost beyond our established boundaries will be under the control of Command," Perro told him. "Team Three is perfect for the job, first because of the Gen En. You're trained in Security, and you're young enough to finish what we start."

"Again, why?"

"That's a simple question with a hard answer." Perro considered how detailed he wanted to explain at this point. "You will accept your nomination in to Command?"

"Yes," Mac said without hesitation.

"Just as Command has its secrets, so does the Council. These clandestine activities have their reasons, of course. Council has concealed things from the public since we established The Vista."

"What sort of things?" Mac was quick to presume.

"The genetically manipulated are little more that rumors from the past. Our concern is other cities, other places like The Vista we recognize are out there, but we have no contact with, out of fear of what might be."

Mac took in his words, a flurry of complications filling his mind. "How many cities? How many people?" For as long as he could remember, The Vista was the only place in the world, and its few thousand people, the only ones he'd ever known.

"We estimate there are thirty thousand people within a summer's traveling distance of here."

A generation ago, there had been six billion humans–a number Mac couldn't even fathom. Thirty thousand was a different story. "Fear of what?"

"The problem, exactly," Perro repeated, crossing his arms. MacKenzie might not be the quiet one, but he was just as sharp as Wade and, he suspected, as dangerous. "Fear that the things causing the war are still happening. Fear that there will be enemies rather than allies. We won't be able to control everything here if there is outside influence. This last incident, this attack by forces that may or may not have been military-trained people, it might be backlash from the war itself. The detonation on the Missouri Breaks, too. We don't know. These are the reason for our caution and our concern."

"We've never had control," Mac said, puzzled by the idea of it.

"No," Perro agreed. "And that is why Command wants you and your team. You'll be our defense, our protection, even more than you are now."

Mac didn't see another choice for the immediate future.

* * * * *

"You don't realize how isolated it is out here until you spend a few days with nothing to do," Wade said, looking out over the Station from a hillside to the north. His horse stomped, restless. Beside him, Shan took in the view, glad to be out for a few hours. They both were still healing, but the warm, cloudless morning had called to them.

"I like the quiet here," she said.

"The privacy."

"Yes. I want to see my parents, but this is safer for us."

He glanced at her, sensing a deeper meaning in her words. "Don't let 'safe' be a word you're comfortable with. I don't see it in our stars."

She nodded, "I agree."

"And stop agreeing with everything I say."

"Fine. Shut up. I disagree," she smiled back at him. They were both wrapped in heavy winter gear. It snowed the day before, it was going to happen again soon.

"With what?"

"Everything."

"I'm serious. I've said it before. If you think I'm mistaken about anything, speak up," he pursued the idea. "You're part of my team. I don't want you to follow along and say 'yes' to me because you expect you should. Make your own judgment."

"You know I do. Why the lecture now?" Shan couldn't imagine challenging him, not in front of others. Mac, maybe.

"Because now you're an officer, not a trainee. We put you in the middle of the worst incidents we've had in years."

"I got myself shot."

He paused. They'd lost six officers and no civilians. "You did. So did I. Not the point. We're Team Three. Command might not be aware of what we are. They might know everything. Don't expect it to be a secret forever."

"What do we do, when and if?"

"If they accuse us of being what we are? Not a concern for you. I created the 'Conda with various purposes in mind."

"Okay. I trust that. You."

"What is it you've been thinking and won't talk about in the Station?"

It didn't surprise her that he sensed her unease. "Pick a subject."

"Mac," he said, holding up a gloved hand before she replied. "You don't have to tell me a thing. Be careful is all I ask. What else?"

"The helicopters."

"We took them both down."

"Where did they come from? Are there more of them? And were they looking for us?"

He didn't have an answer to any of her questions. Wade smiled, glad winter was setting in. It would give them all time to recover and to consider the same questions. The change he'd been looking for as long as he could remember was coming. It wouldn't be easy, but few things were. "Someday, I hope soon, we're going to venture out into the world and see what there is. Maybe we'll find answers. You're welcomed to join us."

Out in the world. Shan liked the idea. "I'm ready when you are."

* * * * *

~end of this one, beginning of the story arc~

For more -

The Wildblood Series

Backlash: Prequel to The Wildblood

Trilogy 1

The Vista: Book 1 of The Wildblood
Renegades: Book 2 of The Wildblood
Bloodlines: Book 3 of The Wildblood

novellas

Outliers: Team Two
Outliers: Texas

More to come!

The Vista: Book 1 of The Wildblood

A Post-Apocalyptic Action Adventure

World War Last pushed humanity to the brink of extinction.

Cut off from the chaos of a pandemic mutated by nuclear war, a group of survivors gathered in a secluded mountain valley. Those that lived through the winter founded The Vista.

Twenty years on, their children are guardians of the hidden enclave. A dark secret, that a few of them are different, something of urban legend, draws them together to protect their home. Venturing out into the world will be more dangerous than anything they've faced.

What they are might save them. It could destroy them. Their enemies know.

* * * * *

Also by S. A. Hoag

On another world, in another time, there is -
Tau Scorpii: The Myth of SolTerra

Left to live or die on their own, scattered Terran clans struggle against the elements, other species, and each other. They don't know how or why they're on Sedna, a massive, nearly barren world on the edge of dual solar systems. It's about to get even more difficult to survive. The weather is changing, and no one knows what's next. A group of warriors must make peace with each other while looking for clues to their past and answers about their future. The alternative is extinction.

About the Author

S. A. Hoag is an author, artist, and amateur astronomer ("I just look at the stars, I can't tell you their names."). Born in the middle of the Rocky Mountains of Colorado, she has lived in a number of cities, in a number of states, and is off on another adventure when not writing or creating other art. Science Fiction has always been her first interest in reading and writing. Many other genres sneak into the novels and that's all right with her.

www.topaz08.com

Made in the USA
Monee, IL
07 April 2025

15286942R00069